Ba

A New Adult Romance

by Elizabeth Nelson

Contents

CHAPTER 1

"Kerri, I'm going to kill you." I gripped the back of my best friend's pants as we wound our way through the sweaty, drunk crowd dancing to the pulsing music.

"No you won't, Sasha. This is going to be fun," Kerri said over her shoulder, her voice way too chirpy for the amount of alcohol in her system.

I pressed my lips together and twisted out of the way of another pair of grabbing hands. I didn't hate parties, or loud music, or even drinking. But after six nights, I was ready for a quiet night in.

Alone.

"You've got to hear this band, then we'll go," Kerri shouted.

No, I don't, I thought. I can do without ever hearing another garage band.

Kerri stopped and I ran into her back. The crowd pressed into the gap behind me and I bristled. A smelly tidal wave of alcohol and perfume crashed over me and I tried breathing through my mouth but it didn't taste much better than it smelled. "Ten minutes, Kerri, then I'm going home."

Kerri tugged me beside her. "Fine. Ten minutes."

I sighed and settled in for an hour of terrible lyrics and a complete lack of musicality. No matter what I threatened Kerri, I would never leave her alone. Above us, the band members mingled around the stage, moving equipment and sound checking. An opened bottle of Jack Daniels sat in front of the drum set and cigarette smoke lent a ghostly quality to the set.

How they could possibly hear anything over the other music blaring through the party was beyond me. Kerri leaned closer and whispered, "The one in the black shirt is Jesse. He's their lead singer and writes all their stuff."

Super. I didn't roll my eyes. "How do you know him?"

"He played Trey's frat party last week."

I'd been lucky to escape that one. My chemistry professor made me retake a quiz. Now I was wishing she had seven other quizzes. The front-man, Jesse, turned around and I narrowed my eyes. *I think he's in my English class.* Not that it mattered—after tonight Jesse and his band would be a bad memory.

Kerri twisted away and waved frantically. I peered over her shoulder. Kerri's boyfriend, Trey, lifted the four beer bottles in salute and weaved through the crowd. He handed us each a bottle, took a swig of one and set the remaining bottle on the stage. Jesse sauntered over and crouched down, legs splayed on either side of my head. *Nice cock shot, creep. Ugh.*

I angled my head so I could stare past his crotch. His straight dark hair fell over one eye, adding a dark edge to his Asian features. I took another step back and studied Jesse while he talked to Trey. Straight dark brows accented almond eyes that roamed the crowd. They landed on me and I met his stare. His full lips curved up in a cocky smile and he clinked his beer against mine. Foam raced toward the lip. Without comment or grimace, I lifted it to my lips and swallowed. All the girls probably simpered and flirted at that look.

Well, they weren't me.

"Thanks for coming," Jesse said, still looking at me. Alcohol lowered his lids seductively, but all I could see was a drunk. He was wasted. Or stoned.

"Yeah. Kerri made me."

Kerri made a face and threw her hands up. She'd made it her mission this semester to hook me up. A plan that was doomed to fail.

Jesse took a pull off his beer. "Maybe I'll see you around."

I smiled to make Kerri happy, but didn't put much effort into it.

"Thanks for the drink," he said to Trey.

"Yeah man, catch you after."

Someone killed the blaring pop track and heads swiveled toward the stage. Bodies pressed closer, cocooning me in a smothering warmth. The drummer tapped out a beat, then Jesse jumped into the song. They were semi-talented and I didn't actually hate the track. It wasn't anything I'd add to a playlist, and if they'd get rid of the bass player, it would be better. Jesse could sing and seemed to have some skill with the guitar. An impressive feat, considering how smashed he was. Sober he was probably incredibly talented.

I relaxed and sipped my beer. Then winced. I should have asked Trey for an apple martini or cosmopolitan. Beer hated me and I'd have a gut ache before long. Jesse started up a new set and my finger tapped the label.

Damn.

I really didn't want to like this punk's music. He smiled and stared at me during the entire song. He was probably so used to groupies throwing random clothes his way after singing a song to them.

Sorry bub, my panties don't work like that.

I broke his gaze and scanned the crowd. Dozens of chicks were gyrating and yelling. Yep, there's the first pair of panties. A pink thong sailed through the air and landed at the keyboardist's feet. He grinned and blew a kiss at the redhead who'd basically tossed her vagina on stage.

I rolled my eyes and glanced at Jesse. His grin widened and he winked.

Oh no, I'm not falling for that either. I ignored him and took another drink. As he started the next song, my foot joined my tapping finger and I admitted that they were actually very talented. Not that I'd tell him that. Or Kerri. God, that girl needed absolutely no ammunition when it came to boys.

The band played three more original songs, then a couple covers. I hid my smile behind my bottle when they played my favorite Kansas song. No way even a dozen of these drunks knew who Kansas was. Jesse caught my attention and winked again. I raised an eyebrow but didn't look away this time. His grin widened and he gyrated his hips.

I laughed. *Okay, maybe he's funny, but that doesn't mean I'm interested.*

Kerri tugged on my arm. "Still going to kill me?"

"Shut it."

"Admit it, you're having a good time."

I pressed my cheek against Kerri's. "Like I'd tell you."

Kerri grinned and bounced up and down. "I knew it!"

I pretend-glared.

Kerri wiggled her hips. "Trey wants us to come back to the frat house."

I bunched my lips and wrinkled my nose. There really wasn't anything I could use for an excuse. For the first time in a month, I was totally caught up on my homework. My next test wasn't for another two weeks, and the office where I temped was getting remodeled. I actually had nothing going on.

And Kerri knew it.

I nodded, making Kerri squeal and jump up and down.

"It's just a party. Not a date!"

Kerri wiggled her eyebrows.

"I'm serious Kerri. I am not dating that boy." I pointed my beer at Jesse. And groaned.

I didn't realize he'd just finished a song while Kerri had been teasing me. With my arm outstretched, I looked like a complete groupie. He grinned and blew me a kiss. Every girl within a ten-foot radius sighed and reached up to catch it.

"He's totally into you."

"He's totally into Jack Daniels, right now. I'm just another pair of panties."

"Thanks for coming everyone," Trey said as he popped the microphone into the holder. "Come see us at Port O'Call, next week. Goodnight!"

Wild applause erupted and they exited stage left.

Trey slipped a hand around Kerri's waist. "Ready, you two?"

Kerri leaned up and whispered in his ear. Trey looked at me, jumped his gaze up at the stage, then back. He raised an eyebrow. "Really?"

"No," I said. "Not *really*. Whatever she told you is a typical Kerri-exaggeration. I'm coming to the frat house. That's *it*."

Trey shrugged and gave her a lopsided grin. "Sure. Whatever you say."

"Kerri," I drew out the word. "Stop telling him lies."

"Sure," she chirped. "Whatever you say."

I shook my head and rolled my eyes, following them out of the party.

We walked down the block to the frat house with Trey and Kerri mauling each other the whole way. I was used to their public displays of affection, so it didn't bother me. What did bug me was that I couldn't get that damn band's songs out of my head. I'd been humming one for the last hundred yards.

Trey's hand slipped up Kerri's shirt. That was a new one. "Get a room you two."

"Almost there," Trey said before jamming his tongue down Kerri's throat.

I jogged ahead of them and up the frat house steps. Axel greeted me at the door. I kissed his dark cheek and slipped an arm through his. "Make me a drink?"

"Of course." Axel kissed the tip of my nose. His hazel eyes hinted at something more, like always, but he'd been relegated to the friend zone since the moment we met. He was too kind, too wonderful for me to ruin with a relationship. He'd asked me out at least a dozen times, but finally quit last year after I'd told him that he couldn't hang out with me anymore if he didn't stop.

But he still gave me this wounded puppy look every time he saw me.

I bumped my hip against his. "Dating anyone?"

He twisted his head and looked down at me. "No one worth having."

I scowled. "I'll work on finding you someone."

"No need. I've already found her, just waiting for her to get her head out."

I yanked on his arm. "Better stop."

"You said I couldn't hit on you, not that I couldn't bring it up."

"You can't bring it up."

"Too late."

Axel turned and pressed his back into the swinging door that led to the kitchen. His arms wound around my waist. "Oops."

I laughed and smacked his arm. "You're impossible."

"And relentless." He wound his fingers through mine and tugged me toward the mini-bar set up on the counter. "What'll it be?"

"Cosmo?"

"Hmmm." He pretended to examine the bottles, shaking his head and setting each one down. "What's in that again?"

"Vodka, triple sec, lime, and cranberry juice."

"Ah yes, girly, wimpy, hardly alcoholic."

"On purpose!" I teased. "Like I'd ever get wasted around here. That's a good way to get date raped."

Axel's face fell. "I'd never let that happen."

I tipped my head to the side and touched his forearm. "I know. But still."

"But still. Probably a good personal rule."

I wagged my finger. "Boys can get date raped too, you know."

"I wish!"

I laughed and planted my hands on my hips. "You're—"

"Relentless. Yes, we went over this." He leaned forward and kissed my nose right as I tipped my chin to correct him. Our lips met. His were warm and firm. A strong hand instantly encircled my waist and pulled me closer.

"Sorry," a voice said from the doorway.

I spun. Jesse stood in the doorway. I glanced at Axel and walked out of the kitchen.

"Sash—" Music drowned out the rest of Axel's sentence.

I pressed my fingertips to my lips. They tingled and I had a queasy feeling that if Jesse hadn't interrupted, I wouldn't have pushed Axel away. God, I must be ovulating. First, a rockstar-wannabe was infiltrating my thoughts and now my best friend was getting me bothered.

Swinging around the railing, I ran upstairs and knocked on Trey's door. "Kerri, I'm headed out."

Muffled voices and moaning stopped. "Wait," Kerri said through the door. Then Trey mumbled something.

"Are you okay?" Kerri pulled the door open a crack. She held a sheet to her chest. Naked shoulders and a wild halo of hair made my guts twist. They hadn't wasted any time getting busy.

"Yeah, I just got tired."

"What happened?"

I shook my head. This would take longer than Kerri could give me right now. "I'm fine. We'll talk tomorrow."

Kerri narrowed her eyes. "Are you lying?"

"No!" I pulled my fake grin wider. "Seriously. I'm fine."

Kerri blew me a kiss. "Text me when you get home."

"Trey," I yelled over Kerri's head. "Don't let her walk home alone."

"Never."

I waved my fingers and turned. The door clicked and Kerri squealed. This time I rolled my eyes. Trey was a good guy, but certainly not permanent material. I managed to dodge Axel and slipped through the bodies and out the front door.

"Hey," a voice called behind me.

At the bottom step, I turned. Jesse stood at the edge of the patio, hands jammed in his jean pockets. "Can I give you a ride?"

"No, thanks. Not a fan of getting in cars with drunks." Bodies shifted and morphed behind Jesse like a kaleidoscope backdrop. So far, I didn't see Axel.

"I'm not drunk."

I raised an eyebrow. *I do not have time for this.* "Right."

"No seriously. I drank before the show—," he hesitated. "A lot. But playing in front of a crowd is such a rush I burn it all." He held up a flat hand. "See? Stone-cold sober."

"Still not getting in a car with you. Thanks."

"Can I walk you?"

I shook my head. As I turned, Axel's head popped over the crush of people. Damn. He would totally follow me and want to talk about what happened. I didn't need things getting any weirder tonight. I glanced at Jesse and tried to size him up. Creep or overconfident guitarist?

He shrugged and turned toward the house. Axel was almost to the door.

"Fine," I shouted.

Jesse looked over his shoulder, one eyebrow raised. "What?"

"Fine. Fine, you can walk me home."

He grinned and jogged down the steps. I ducked my head and sped up. "Come on."

"Sash!" Axel's voice carried across the lawn, but I didn't look back. Jesse paused and jerked his thumb toward the house. "Hey, you need to get that?"

I quickened my pace. "No. Keep walking."

Jesse caught up. "So did you like the show?"

"It was okay."

He laughed. "Seriously? Just okay. You're a tough sell."

"The Kansas cover was nice."

"Wondered if anyone caught that."

"I'm a music snob, just so you know."

"Like you only listen to classical or something?"

I squeezed my eyes and shook my head. We rounded the corner of the block and I slowed. "No, like I know good music and don't listen to crap."

"So I guess I should be glad you stayed."

"Kerri made me."

"She seems cool."

I stopped. "You don't need to walk me the rest of the way."

Jesse held up his hands. "Okay, she's *not* cool."

"I just needed you to get me out of there. I can walk the rest of the way by myself."

"Nope." He jutted his chin forward. "My moral code insists I walk all damsels in distress all the way to their doors."

Ugh. Creep-alert. I sighed and started walking again. "Whatever."

"We have Lit together, right?"

"Mr. Wracks."

Jesse tapped my shoulder. "Yeah. You always sit in the front. Are you a nerd?"

"I showed up late on the first day. That was the only seat left. Now it's just habit."

We walked in silence past a few driveways. "So that guy you were kissing. Are you two a thing?"

"No!" I blurted, then recovered. "We're just friends."

"Like friends with—"

"Don't even say it. No, there are no *benefits* of being my friend."

"Okay good, because I wanted to ask you out."

I jerked to a stop and spun to face him. "Are you out of your mind?"

His eyebrows rose in a perfect arc. "I didn't think so. I like you and want to spend more time with you."

I crossed my arms, and narrowed my eyes. "But you'd have settled for friends with benefits?"

He held up his hands, palms out. "No. God no, just didn't want you giving them to that guy."

Jealous much? "I don't date musicians."

Jesse started walking. "Yeah, me neither. So tomorrow night?"

"No." I huffed and followed. "Aren't you listening? No musicians."

"I'm just a guy in your Lit class."

"And a musician."

"I'm sure you have a hobby I won't like. We're a wash."

"Ugh." I threw up my hands. "You're not even listening."

"See? You're kind of a nag, totally cancels out my band."

My eyes widened. "You're already calling me names?"

"You nagged, I merely called you on it. Is Sunday better? We could do lunch."

"We're not going out."

"Breakfast, tomorrow morning. Seven. That's not a date."

I paused at the end of my sidewalk. "You're not going to let up, are you?"

Jesse flashed that irritating all-teeth grin. He tapped his right toe on the sidewalk. "Meet you right here."

"Thanks for walking me."

"My pleasure." He turned and strolled up the sidewalk.

I watched his back until he turned the corner, then shook my head, and went inside.

CHAPTER 2

I rolled over and smacked my alarm clock. Fog clouded my brain. *What class do I have this morning?* I stared at the blinking numbers on the clock. Saturday. Today's Saturday.

I rubbed my eyes, then swung out of bed and pulled my running shoes on. More fog parted and I remembered Kerri texting in the middle of the night. She stayed over but wanted to meet for breakfast at nine.

Plenty of time to get a run in and get ready. I swiped a banana and my iPod off the counter. Jamming the buds into my ears, I jogged down the stairs then sped up when I hit the sidewalk. Easy six-miler today. Clouds covered the sun, lending a gray cast to everything in the neighborhood. Early enough that it wasn't yet hot, but humidity already clung to my skin. A car sped out of a driveway and I hit the hood with my hand as I swerved. "Running here!"

An old man scowled from behind the wheel.

"Yeah, back at ya, bub."

I bounded off the sidewalk and into the road. This section with its cracks and heaved pavement always made me nervous about rolling an ankle. But the narrow road and parked cars gave me the freaks. No one ever looked, obviously.

Another block passed. I leaned forward and sped up. Blood pumped through my thighs and air filled my lungs. Today was a good day. Maybe even good enough to beat my personal best. One more block down.

At the light, I pressed the crosswalk button and jogged in place. I wasn't winded at all, and right here was usually when I started feeling a twinge. The cross-traffic light turned yellow and I scanned the opposite sidewalk. A runner in a hoodie moved steadily toward the intersection. He'd get there right about when the light changed. My walk light flashed white and I took off. Out of habit, I smiled at the runner as I went by.

My feet stuttered. A familiar grin lit up beneath the hood. I kept running.

"Wait up," Jesse called. The entrance to the park beckoned less than twenty feet away. I surged forward. He gained. Footsteps intruded over my music. I swung right into the entrance and he materialized at my side. "Great day for a run."

"Go away." I sped up but he matched me again. I slowed and he did.

I glanced sideways, but he stared straight ahead, comfortable at my pace.

Fine. We'll see how long he can stick with me. The path curved downward and to the left. I lengthened my stride and sped up. Jesse didn't fall back an inch. My chest tightened as I reached my max speed. Jesse's relaxed face made him look like he was out for an afternoon stroll. Of all the people to be a runner.

I finished the lap and slowed to a jog.

"You're fast. What's your best mile?" He wasn't even winded.

"Nine, five." I gasped like a landed fish.

His eyebrows lifted. "Nice."

Even though I didn't want to, I asked anyway. "Yours?"

"Eight, fifteen."

I grunted. No chance of ever ditching him then. A bench sat tucked back beneath two oak trees and marked my six miles. I stopped and sat. As expected,

Jesse plopped down and stretched his arms along the back. Blood surged through my thighs, making them tingle. I leaned forward and stretched my hamstrings.

"Where do you want to eat breakfast?"

"Already with that?"

Jesse tugged a lock of my ponytail. "It's just food, Sasha. You can't run and not eat."

I huffed. His annoying suggestion wouldn't be so bad if I had anything in the fridge. Grocery shopping day was Sunday, and since we went out Friday and most of Saturday, it worked.

Until today.

"Fine. Waffle House."

"Really? Wow, I totally figured you for Pesto's or Jinnie's. Somewhere totally granola and organic. Waffle House—that's sweet."

"First you call me a nag, and now you're making fun of my eating habits?"

"Totally not making fun. I love it. Women never eat around me. Especially on dates."

"One. This is not a date. Two. I just ran six miles. Granola is not going to work."

He wrapped his arms around my shoulders and tugged me hard against his side. "Woman after my own heart."

I wrestled my way out of his grasp and stood. Balancing one hand against the back of the bench, I stretched out my thighs. Though I'd never admit it, today *had* been nice with someone pushing me. Maybe next time I'd make Kerri go.

"Do you need to go home, or should we jog down the street?"

"Not a date, so I don't need to primp."

"Well, you look beautiful." Jesse turned and walked toward the Waffle House.

I ducked my head, frustrated at the heat in my cheeks. No matter what Jesse said, there was no way I was falling for him. He had disaster written all over him. At the Waffle House, he held the door, and pulled out my chair.

I set my menu aside and leaned forward. Over the top of his, Jesse's head moved back and forth as he scanned the selection. His head paused and he lowered the menu just enough for me to see his questioning brows.

His eyebrows rose. "You already decide?"

"This is not a date."

He lifted the menu back up.

I sighed and glanced at the inside of the first page. Triple threat—sausage, waffles, eggs. I got it every time. If he wanted to see me eat, then he was in for a treat.

The waitress brought waters and we ordered. I folded my hands on the table and looked out the window.

"What's your favorite class?" Jesse asked.

I tipped my head. "Design studio."

He mimicked my head tilt. "Like painting?"

"No. Landscape architecture."

He stroked his chin. "Interesting. I'm learning all kinds of things about you."

I opened my mouth, but he didn't let me interrupt. "I'm so glad this isn't a date."

I settled back against my chair. "What's yours?"

"Cross Border Mergers & Acquisitions."

"Business?"

"Finance."

"So, when you're not rocking out, you're going to be sporting a suit and tie?" I laughed. "Not seeing it."

"I clean up really nice," he said, sounding mildly offended. "And I have to do something until the gigs take off. My parents wouldn't pay tuition otherwise."

"Fair enough." I crossed my arms across my stomach, retreating from the conversation. Did every musician think it was just a matter of time before they hit the big time? My ex's delusions about it were why I broke it off. Well, that and when I told him to stop dreaming. My heart twisted. I could be such a bitch sometimes.

A bike raced past our window, crossed the street, and sped down the other side.

I had good reasons before my ex for not dating musicians, but he'd only solidified my feelings.

The waitress refilled our coffee. I added more cream until the black coffee turned tan. I cradled it between both hands and pressed my lips against the rim. Jesse slouched against his chair.

"Do you have brothers or sisters?"

I shook my head. "Nope, just me." I took a sip of the coffee. "And my mom."

Jesse blinked, but didn't ask about my dad. His features softened and he smiled. "I have two older brothers and a little sister."

The apples of his cheeks lifted and a tiny dimple appeared beneath his right eye. I hadn't seen that before, even when he'd teased and laughed. *He must be close to his family*. "What's that like having a big family?"

"Awesome and awful at the same time. We're always on top of each other. My sister is a complete princess, very tiny and breakable. She's had us all wrapped around my finger since she showed up. My brothers are loud and obnoxious, but chill. My parents are big fans of the family trip, so our summers were packed with camping and boating."

"I've never been camping."

He leaned forward. "Ever?"

I shook my head. "Nope."

He chuckled. "It's fun. Our family is crazy, we don't do regular campgrounds. My dad loved finding the most obscure places that barely had a road."

"Did that freak your mom out?" I couldn't imagine camping in a KOA, let alone the middle of the wilderness. So not on my bucket list.

"Nah, she usually helped him plan where we were going. My sister hated it though. Dirt does not mix well with her."

I smiled and set my coffee cup down.

"This one time," Jesse braced his hands on the table and laughed, "we were swimming in a natural hot spring and my older brother, Stu, found a huge strand of this kelp-seaweed stuff. He's a complete jokester and lives to freak Miranda out. My mom had barely convinced her to get in the pool and that it wouldn't ruin her new pink suit. She was swimming and Stu came up behind her and pretended the seaweed was a monster attacking him." He laughed hard enough to disturb the nearby tables. "She screamed, and swam for her life, kicked Stu right in the face and broke his nose."

My hands flew to my mouth. "Oh no!"

He leaned back, barely able to talk he was laughing so hard at the memory. "It was priceless. She didn't talk to him for the rest of the trip."

"Were your parents mad?"

"No. We were trying not to laugh because Miranda was so upset, but it was hysterical. I've never been back there, but I think that was one of my favorite trips."

"Because of the sea monster?"

He chuckled again, unable to quit thinking about the memory. "This little hot spring was surrounded by mountains. It looked like a giant had literally carved a pocket out of the side of the mountain. We went in the middle of summer, so the fields were overflowing with wildflowers. I've never seen anything like it." There was a wistful, genuine tone under the laughter. "I wrote my first song there."

I heard the expectation in his voice. He wanted me to ask him about the song, or for me to blush and ask him to sing it. Very familiar territory. And not anywhere I wanted to trespass again. "Sounds beautiful."

"Very." His eyes pinned me. "I'd like to go back again."

I swallowed and forced myself not to wiggle beneath his scrutiny.

The waitress arrived and set three plates in front of me and one heaping stack of pancakes in front of Jesse. He grinned and grabbed his fork. "Dig in."

I filled every square of my waffle with a methodical precision. I looked up at Jesse and dared him to comment. He kept his face passive and took the syrup bottle, drizzling a spiral over the top of his cakes and down the sides.

Plucking a sausage link, I dipped it into the syrup and bit the warm skin. Flavors flooded my mouth and I licked my lips. Jesse forked a tower of pancakes and a companionable silence descended on the space while we ate. Between bites, he set his silverware on the table and blotted his mouth with a napkin.

Not horrible eating across from a guy with manners.

Truly, there wasn't much about Jesse that was horrible. I sneaked a glance from beneath my lowered lashes. There was no denying his good looks, but I knew a ton of cute guys who weren't funny and entertaining. Jesse didn't have the jacked up home life most bad boys rebelled against, and he seemed to genuinely like his siblings and parents. Too bad about the music thing, but maybe we could just be friends.

My heart twisted. I needed to find Axel today and mend things with that friend before I worried about adding a new one.

I sliced into my waffle and syrup pooled onto my plate. I swirled the waffle bite around and hurried it to my mouth before it dripped. While I chewed, my phone beeped. I wiped my hands and read the text.

Trey is a douche. Where R U? flashed on the screen from Kerri.

"Everything okay?" Jesse asked.

"Kerri and Trey must have had a fight this morning." I looked around for the waitress. "I need to get this to go."

Jesse flagged a busboy down.

"You don't have to go," I said as I pushed my plate away. "Really."

"It's fine."

No, really. I didn't need him tagging along while I tried to find out what Trey had done now. This was a weekly occurrence for the two of them. All Kerri needed was a little attention and Trey would show up in a few hours with flowers and apologies.

The waitress brought our check and Jesse asked for boxes. She hurried away and I slipped my hand inside my bra for the twenty I kept there when I ran.

Jesse's eyes widened.

"What?"

He cleared his throat and fought a smile. "Nothing."

The waitress boxed our meals and I added another flood of syrup before closing the lid. Jesse's smile broke. "Have you thought about joining a Syrup Anonymous support group?"

I smiled in spite of his teasing. "I have a problem. I freely admit it. That's why I run."

He held up his hands. "Hey, your addiction."

At the register he tried to pay, but I shoved him aside and handed my twenty to the cashier. "Separate checks, please." I glanced over my shoulder. "Not a date."

He winked and I spun around. I was going to have to talk to him about that if we were going to just be friends.

Jesse paid and held the door open. I headed for an empty spot between two cars to cross the parking lot.

"You're starting to rub off on me. Can we just be—" a chunk of the sidewalk crumbled beneath me as I turned. My ankle collapsed. Asphalt shredded my skin and my ankle throbbed. As I landed, the lid of my To-Go box popped open. Waffles and syrup coated the lower half of my leg and the sidewalk beneath. I groaned and grabbed my ankle. Pain radiated outward.

Jesse dropped to the ground beside me, a hand on my shoulder. "Are you okay?"

I slouched against the tire of a red Prius. "No. Not really." I couldn't relax my fingers. They banded tightly around my ankle, whitening the skin beneath.

"Let me see." Jesse covered my fingers.

I groaned and dropped my head back, squeezing my eyes shut tight. "It's fine."

"It's not fine." He pried my fingers away and grunted.

Strands of syrup clung to my hands. The view tilted. I squeezed my eyes tighter. "What's that mean?"

"You need a doctor."

I squinted and opened one eye. While I'd been sitting there, my ankle had grown to twice the size. I couldn't even see my ankle bone anymore. But I could feel it. It screamed and twisted in my leg. Jesse squeezed my fingers gently. I didn't realize he'd been holding my hand. "Do you want me to call an ambulance?"

I grimaced. "No. God, no. Just help me back to my place."

He kneeled next to me and plucked the waffles off my shoe. "I think you're breakfast is a goner." Thick rivers of syrup dripped off the waffle and into my shoe. "I promise I'm not bad luck."

I pressed upward, leveraging my shoulder against the car's fender. Jesse supported my arms until I was upright. *Of all the people to have to rely on*. The parking lot spun again and I gripped his hand. One arm slipped around my waist. "I got you."

The ground flattened out and I sagged against his chest. "I'm okay, just give me a sec."

Jesse didn't release his hold. I shifted my weight, and touched my toe to the ground. Pain shrieked up my entire leg, wobbling the cars and asphalt again. My stomach lurched.

"No good." Jesse leaned forward, slipped one hand behind my knees, and scooped me into his arms.

Everything spun and I clutched his shoulders. He looked at me and waited. "You're green."

"I'm okay." My head fell against his shoulder. Strong arms tightened around my back.

"Let's get you home." Jesse shifted my weight. Another wave of nausea forced my eyes closed. I linked my hands behind his neck and concentrated on not feeling every single one of his steps pulsing through my ankle.

On the other side of the street, his breathing came harder and faster.

"I'm probably heavy."

His gaze wandered over me and he smiled. "Light as a feather."

I squirmed and he cradled me closer against him. He smelled minty with a hint of bacon and maple syrup. I studied my knees. Beneath them, my skin tingled where his arms held me.

A dog lunged from behind a shrub, barking and growling. Jesse twisted away, bumping my toe on a mailbox. Pain eclipsed my vision and stole my breath.

I wanted to scream but squeezed Jesse's neck and buried my face into his shoulder instead.

"I'm sorry. Sorry." He pressed his cheek against mine. Either he was trembling, or I was. He held me tighter and doubled his speed. "We're almost there. Hang on."

I did. My arms ached with the grip around his neck. If a whisper of a touch like the mailbox was enough to make it hurt this bad, there's no way this was something that would heal quickly.

Jesse slowed and I glanced up. We'd finally made it to my house. Kerri raced down the steps, arms outstretched. Who knows how long she'd been outside waiting for me to get home.

"Wait!" Jesse yelled. "I think her ankle's broken."

Kerri's hands flew to her mouth. "Oh, Sash." She stepped aside so Jesse could carry me in.

"Wait a minute, were you guys together?" Kerri looked from Jesse to me as he lowered me to the couch.

"I met her while she was running."

Kerri kneeled next to the couch and smoothed my hair back from my forehead. "Do I need to take you to the hospital?"

Jesse paced. "Yes. Immediately. I'd take her but I don't have a car."

I looked up drowsily. "You don't have a car?"

He glanced away. "No."

"I can take her." Kerri raced to the counter and scooped up her keys. "But can you get her in?"

"Advil," I croaked.

Kerri tossed her keys from one hand to the other. "Sash, I think you need to call your mom."

"No way." I shot up from my prone position on the couch. "Absolutely not."

"Are you sure? I mean if you have to go the hospital we're going to need insurance. They're going to ask you all kinds of questions.

"I said no, Kerri."

Jesse stepped outside while we argued. A golden flame glowed in the gray morning, then ignited the tip of his cigarette. I glared at him through the wall then back at Kerri. "Please don't call her, Ker."

"Fine. Jesse, will you carry her?" He stomped out the cigarette and blew a huge cloud of smoke that floated above his head and into the house.

"Yeah." He scooped me up off the couch, gentle fingers belying his rough edges. Cigarette smoke clung to his skin and clothes. I wrinkled my nose. He smelled awful.

He followed Kerri outside and settled me into the back, gently lifting both feet onto the seat and buckling the seatbelt around my hips.

"Thanks. I guess I'll see you later," I said.

He shut the door and ran around the front of the car, slipping into the passenger seat. Kerri adjusted the mirror and smirked at me in the reflection. "We'll have to carry you in," Kerri told me before I could ask. I rolled my eyes at her and glared. She didn't know what she was playing at, but obviously finding us together for breakfast had led her to the wrong conclusion. I leaned my head against the window.

"What happened with Trey?"

"Ugh, he's such a jerk." She started the engine and backed out of our small parking lot.

"He's always a jerk, Kerri. I've told you that from the day you started dating him."

"Well this time it was worse."

I glanced at her in the mirror. She wasn't making eye contact. I knew she didn't want to hear what I had to tell her. She never wanted to hear it. I wasn't sure how much I could berate her with Jesse in the car, though, clearly listening.

"What happened?" he asked.

Kerri's glaze flicked to me in the rearview mirror. She sighed. "After you left, he started drinking and got into a fight with boys from another house. I bailed and walked home even though he promised to give me a ride." I kept my mouth shut. She didn't want to hear me lecture her now because that was the stupidest thing she could have done. By that time, she'd probably had more to drink than she could have handled and her 'I'm staying over' text was at two, so by the time they fought, it would have been late and dark. Fine for me to walk it alone but I'd been mostly sober.

"That was pretty dumb," Jesse voiced my concern.

Kerri sighed. "I know but I was mad."

"Still that was dumb. You girls should call me when you need an escort."

This time I did roll my eyes. Kerri saw me and giggled. "Sasha sure made it home safe."

"He dropped me at the door Kerri." Jesse didn't bother to corroborate my story. I glared at the back of his head.

Kerri swung us into a front spot at the hospital, tipping me sideways and banging my toe against the back of the seat. I moaned.

Jesse was around the car and opening my door before the pain made me pass out. "I got you," he whispered. I didn't like that he'd been saying that a lot since my injury. I didn't want him to *have* me. He still smelled like cigarette smoke. I hated that too.

Strong fingers slid beneath my ribs while he eased me backward on the seat until he could get his other arm beneath my knees. He lifted me easily and held me against his chest. My arms naturally went around his neck.

"Don't think I didn't see that little smirk," I said, linking my hands tighter.

"A smirk doesn't mean anything. This still isn't a date. I'm just carrying you." Kerri shut the door and ran ahead to open the hospital's double doors.

Inside, I answered the nurse's barrage of questions and she finally led me into a small, glass-walled cube. Jesse eased me onto the bed and the nurse adjusted the head so I could lean back. "Thanks, you can go now," I told Jesse.

"Or stay," he said, landing in the only open chair. I could hear Kerri outside my room on the phone, probably with my mother.

"No really," I said, adjusting myself higher on the bed. "Don't you have a concert to get ready for or something?"

Jesse leaned back in the chair and crossed one ankle over his knee. "Nope. Next gig isn't for a week."

Great.

Kerri hung up and peeked around the curtain. "Everybody decent?"

I chuckled. Jesse stood and offered her the chair but a nurse came in behind Kerri with another. "I thought you guys could use this."

"Thanks." Jesse took it from her and settled it on the other side of my bed. Too close for my comfort. I inched closer to Kerri's side. Jesse situated the chair until he was at an angle, then rested his forearm on the bed next to mine. If I scooted further away now, it would be obvious he was making me uncomfortable. I wasn't about to give him the satisfaction.

"So what's the deal with Trey now?" he asked, leaning forward until our skin accidentally touched. A shock of warmth flashed up my arm. "Are you guys over?"

Kerri lowered herself to the chair and sighed. "I don't know. He's such a pain but he can be so nice. I don't know. He's been apologizing for the last six hours at thirty-minute intervals. I want to take him back just so he'll stop bugging me."

I laughed. "That's so Trey."

"I know, right?" she said with a wistful look in her eyes.

"What is it with girls? What is the attraction to a guy who treats them like crap?" Jesse asked.

Kerri bristled. "He doesn't always treat me like crap."

"Okay, if he ever treats you like crap, that's one time too many. You deserve respect, not crap."

I blinked. Who was he to be giving relationship advice? Mr. Smoker-Drinker-Panties-on-the-Stage-Rockstar. *Please*. I knew all too well how that life played out.

He leaned forward and braced his other arm on the bed. "No, I'm serious. I don't understand what this attraction is. I know better than anyone what girls will do for a guy who pretends to be a bad boy."

I scoffed. "Pretends? So this is an act you have, this bad boy rocker?"

He shifted his gaze to mine and held it. "I don't know. I've been doing it for so long I'm not sure anymore." He snapped his mouth shut. "We were talking about Kerri." He broke the stare. "Kerri, I don't know you very well but you seem like a nice girl. If Trey doesn't treat you like he should, you need to dump his ass."

Tears flooded her eyes and she looked away. I couldn't stop staring at the side of Jesse's head. Who was he? "You totally perpetuate the attitude," I told him, returning to his life rather than Kerri's.

He leaned back in his chair and crossed his arms over his chest. "How do you figure?"

"Oh my gosh. Are you serious? Hello. You take home how many different girls a night? Your entire band is completely surrounded by groupies all the time." My ankle throbbed and the room tilted. I gulped air and leaned my head back. Oh, I hate musicians. Hate them.

"Sasha, that's not very nice," Kerri said, scooting her chair closer to the bed in case she needed to intervene.

"Okay, you cannot tell me you're sticking up for him."

"I'm not sticking up but there's no need to be rude. He's been very helpful."

Jesse watched our volley without comment.

A nurse pushed through the curtain. "Okay, let's get some vitals." She flopped half a dozen plastic packages on the tray at the end of my bed. "First some blood pressure." She pulled a cuff out of the first plastic bag. Jesse eased his chair to the foot of the bed, settling his warm fingers around my knee. It tickled but I couldn't yank it away without cracking him in the chin or bumping my broken ankle. Though right now, I wouldn't mind busting him one in the chin.

The nurse pulled out an oxygen monitor and wrapped the sticky sides around my finger. She checked the monitor, took my temperature, and squeezed my shoulder. "What'd you do, hun?"

"She fell off a curb," Jesse said.

I widened my eyes and gave him the visual what-are-you-doing look.

"That's nice your friends came, hun," the nurse said, entering details into the computer. "That ankle looks pretty bad. Do you think it's broken?"

I stared at my giant, swollen ankle. "Not sure. I've never broken a bone before."

"Really?" Jesse's fingertips made circles on the skin at the back of my knee. We still hadn't had that 'just friends' conversation. I needed to hurry that up. Apparently, holding me in his arms three separate times was enough for him to think touching me was okay.

"The doctor will be right in, hun." The nurse bustled out and I let out a breath.

I couldn't remember where I'd left off with these two. Jesse didn't seem like he was in any big hurry to start the conversation again. He reversed the direction of the circles. I wiggled my leg, "Stop that."

"What?"

"Stop touching me."

He lifted his fingers away from my knee but didn't take his hand off my leg. "Seriously, Jesse, we're not dating—ever."

"I know, I know, we're just running buddies. I was massaging your leg."

"That's not a massage."

"I'll totally give you a good massage when we get home. This was just the precursor."

I relaxed into the bed and let my eyes drift closed. Kerri's phone chirped. I could almost see her smile from behind my lids.

"Now what's Trey saying?" I asked.

"He just dropped roses off at the house and wants to know if I want to go to dinner with him tonight."

Jesse's fingers tightened on my leg. "Are you going to go?"

I opened one eye. Kerri shrugged. "I was kind of thinking about what you said. Maybe we should take a break for a while."

I closed my eyes. Was she really going to do it?

"He kind of seems to have your number if all he has to do is text you and take you out for food and you forgive his jackassness." I hated to admit it, but Jesse's hard lining was full of things I'd wanted to say to her for a long time. I hadn't because the one time I'd hinted at how I felt, she hadn't spoken to me for a week. Two good things might come of this: getting rid of Jesse if he pissed Kerri off enough, or getting rid of Trey.

"I know." She drew the word out like taffy.

"Do you want me to do it?" Jesse leaned around the bed, arm outstretched.

Kerri jerked her phone out of reach. "I can do it."

"Go ahead, I'll watch."

Their playful banter confused me. In public and at parties, Kerri played Sorority Girl pretty well. In private, she was completely different, preferring to read, study, and solve the unsolvable math problems. Normally, she wouldn't be listening to Jesse, let alone considering his suggestions. Clearly, he had a way with women. I'm not sure why I was surprised Kerri wasn't immune to his charms.

My guts twisted and I scowled. I didn't like that reaction. *Why should I care if Kerri is interested in Jesse? I'm not.*

Not that he's any better than Trey, and probably worse. I hadn't seen him get into a fistfight yet, and that was Trey's M.O.

Jesse had plenty of demons. What Kerri needed was a sweet, gentle, nice guy like Axel. "Oh my gosh!" I sat up straight. "Kerri, I forgot to talk to you about what happened last night at the party."

She snapped her phone shut. "Why you left?"

"Yes." I smacked my hand to my forehead. "I accidently kissed Axel."

Jesse's fingers tightened on my leg again. Not panicked, like when Kerri said she was calling Trey, but possessive.

"How do you accidently kiss someone?" Kerri asked.

"That was my next question," Jesse added softly, then sat back to listen to our conversation.

"Oh my gosh, you guys, shut up. You know that I kiss him on the cheek all the time."

"And?" Kerri said.

"I accidently moved my face. He tried to kiss me on the nose. Our lips met. It was horrible."

"Horrible, like you didn't enjoy it, or—"

"No, horrible like I kissed Axel. You know he's got a thing for me. Now, he obviously thinks I really have a thing for him."

"Do you have a thing for him?"

"No! God, you're not even listening to me."

"So why'd you kiss him?"

"Kerri, listen. I did not kiss him. I mean, I did kiss him—I did kiss him. But not—I didn't mean to. Our lips, seriously, like ran into each other. But I freaked out because I don't want him getting the wrong idea. I like him. We're friends. It's great. I don't need me blurring the lines—Jesse, get your hand off my leg. Speaking of blurring the lines. We are friends. There is no kissing, touching, fondling—stop fondling my leg."

He held up both hands, "Sorry, sorry."

When he lowered them, one still ended up dangerously close to my calf.

"So what are you going to do?" Kerri asked.

"I don't know. What should I do?"

"Ignore it," Jesse said.

Kerri and I both looked at him.

"Like, not-say-anything ignore it? Or just keep-going-on-like-we-were ignore it?"

He shrugged, "Yeah, just ignore it. If you say anything to him you're going to have to explain how much you loathed the kiss. That's not going to do your friendship any favors. You can't explain it away. Any conversation you try to have about it is just going to call attention to it. Just ignore it."

I lifted one eyebrow, "Why are you being Mr. Helpful all of the sudden?"

One shoulder lifted and fell.

"Axel's cool. I don't think you should go breaking his heart," Kerri added.

"But wouldn't I be leading him on if I don't say anything about it?"

"Not if you don't kiss him again."

The doctor came in, interrupting us.

Was that really the best way to handle it, just to ignore it? Was Jesse right? I didn't want to ruin the relationship I had with Axel. He'd been there for me from the very beginning. I guess I was just going to have to see what happened the next time we were together.

"Does this hurt?"

"Oh yes! Wow—yes!" I gripped the sides of the bed. Jesse covered my fingers with his and I squeezed them.

"Okay, yeah, I'm pretty sure you've broken this." The nurse came in. "Let's get her to X-ray," the doctor requested.

For the next hour, I got transferred from one room to another and back again. Kerri left to go break it off with Trey face-to-face, after Jesse assured her he would make sure I got home. They made the agreement while I was getting my bone set—I'm sure so I couldn't protest.

With a new pink cast encasing my entire left leg, Jesse pushed my wheelchair to the curb. Kerri pulled up as we rolled into the parking lot. She'd been crying.

Jesse loaded me into the car and I leaned forward as far as I could, my fingers brushing Kerri's shoulder and hair. "Are you okay, babe?" I asked her. She shook her head. Tears welled up and dribbled onto her cheeks.

Jesse opened her door. "I'll drive."

She nodded.

With everyone settled, Jesse drove us home and carried me in. He wrote his number on a sticky and set it in the center of the coffee table. "I expect you girls to call me if you need me. I'm an expert pizza, ice cream, and 'chick-flick' delivery boy." Kerri rewarded him with a watery smile.

He ruffled her hair. "You're better off. I promise. I'll be on the lookout for a good guy. Maybe Axel."

I narrowed my eyes at his tone. Why was he trying to setup Axel with Kerri? His reaction to my admission in the hospital still bothered me. He'd seen me kiss him—and it wasn't like we were dating, ever.

"And you, gimpy . . . I'll be escorting you to all your classes this week."

"No thanks, I'm good."

"Haven't you already learned that my chivalry can't be denied?"

He dropped a kiss on my forehead. "Bye, sweet girls."

We watched him walk out, unsure what just happened. Kerri blew her nose, honking loudly into the Kleenex and making us both laugh.

CHAPTER 3

Kerri handed me painkillers and a Coke. "Drink up, sweet cheeks."

I tossed the pill back and took a swig. It burned a trail down my throat. "How long was I out?"

"Couple hours."

"Sorry." I rubbed my forehead and pushed up against the arm of the couch. The kitchen clock dinged four chimes. I'd been out for a few more than a couple. My stomach churned and I burped.

My hand flew to my mouth and Kerri giggled. "Good one."

"Sorry." I laughed and another burp escaped. "Oh my gosh! What is wrong with me?"

"You've been pretty loopy since you got home. You kept laughing in your sleep. Drink some more Coke, this is fun. You're such a prude about it all the time."

Heat flushed my cheeks. Burping was gross. Nearly every memory I had of my dad was him getting into burping contests with his buddies. Back then it was cute for me to do it. I was this tiny, petite thing in dresses burping the National Anthem and the Bad Boys theme song. That all came to a screeching halt when he left. I didn't even allow people to burp around me, which usually made me a raving bitch at parties. Especially frat parties.

I sighed. "Sorry I'm so lame. This is a pretty crappy way to spend a Saturday, taking care of me."

She tossed the remote on the coffee table and raced to my side. "Not true." She brushed hair back from my face. "I can't think of anyone better to spend it with."

I hiccupped and could barely keep my eyes open. She patted my hand and took the can. "I'll set it right here."

I smiled and leaned my cheek against the cushion. Transformers marched across the screen. I watched until the colors blurred then closed my eyes.

The doorbell jarred me.

Kerri eased forward.

"Expecting anyone?" I asked, awake now.

She shook her head. "Trey took it good. I don't think it's him."

We didn't get many visitors. I shrank down on the couch. "If it's Axel, tell him I'm not here."

"I'm sure he heard about your accident by now," she whispered. "And he's probably frantic that you haven't called him."

I waved her away. "Yeah, yeah."

"Hurry!" Jesse's voice called from the other side of the door. "Pizza's getting cold."

My stomach rumbled and my guts twisted. My reactions to him were far from normal.

Kerri opened the door.

"You didn't call, and I was picking up chocolate and pizza and a chick flick for myself tonight. Thought I'd see if you would help me with it."

"Whatever." I laughed. He was persistent, I'd give him that. Sometimes I wished he wasn't a musician. He seemed like he'd be fun to date—I mean, other than the drinking-smoking-panties parts.

He handed the pizza box and movie to Kerri. "Hold on. I have a few more things in my car."

He disappeared from the door and returned a minute later with a six-pack and a huge bouquet of candied roses. He set the beer on the counter, then bowed and gave the flowers to Kerri. "For you."

I smiled. He was pretty charming.

"Thank you," she said with a smile.

"Oops." He plucked one from the middle. "You can't have all of them." He turned and carried it to the couch. Dropping to one knee, he bowed his head and held out the rose. "For you."

I rolled my eyes and bit off half the bud. Strawberry chocolate flooded my mouth and my stomach gurgled.

Jesse stifled a laugh and trailed his fingers gently over my cast. "How's it going?"

I made a face. "We've been a waste of a day, just sitting around. I barely woke up."

"Does it hurt?"

"Only when I move."

He grimaced. "Sorry."

"I suppose everyone should know what a broken bone feels like."

"Can't believe this is your first one."

"Me either," Kerri said, bringing over the pizza, plates, and beer.

I leaned over and slid the movie off the top. "What'd you bring us?" I raised an eyebrow at the title. *"You've Got Mail?* Seriously. You *are* in a chick-flick mood."

"What?" He snatched the box from my fingers. "It's a great movie."

I smiled. "You're a trip."

He popped the movie in and maneuvered me around on the couch, gingerly sliding beneath my legs and settling them on his lap. Again, he had me at a disadvantage—couldn't move without hobbling around, nowhere else to sit. I should have taken the recliner when we got home. At least this time he kept his fingers off my skin.

After polishing off half the pizza, he set his plate down and traced designs across my cast. "We should sign this."

Kerri jumped up. "Oh my gosh—yes! I totally forgot when we got home."

I turned my foot from side to side. "But it's so pretty."

"You can't have a cast without signatures. You'd be a total loser." Kerri handed Jesse a blue marker and she squatted beside the couch, scanning my pink canvas. Resting her hand gently on my ankle, she swooped a big signature and dotted the 'I' with a heart. I laughed.

Jesse pulled the cap off with his teeth and drew a giant heart. I grimaced. He put his initials in the center.

He handed the marker back to Kerri and wiggled out from under my legs. He punched the pause button on the remote. "Be right back."

Kerri leaned over my leg and examined the heart. The front door banged open and closed. She traced the heart. "He's totally into you."

"He carried me home and helped mend your broken heart. That's all."

She shook her head. "No. He's *totally* into you. What guy spends a Saturday night with two chicks watching *You've Got Mail* unless he isn't totally into one?"

That was a pretty good point. I fidgeted. "You know he probably did one of those groupies last night before coming to the party."

She shrugged. "Maybe."

"And I'm not into him, so it doesn't matter."

"What doesn't matter?" Jesse asked, closing the front door and flipping the deadbolt. My nose wrinkled at the smell trailing behind him. He tucked a pack of gum in his back pocket and popped a piece between his teeth.

"That you're nice. That's going to kill you soon anyway."

"Chewing gum?"

I narrowed my eyes. "You know what I mean."

His gaze slid over me, starting at my toes poking out from the tip of the cast, lazily sliding over my legs, pausing for a brief moment on my running shorts, then drifting northward, pausing again at my neck, lips, and eyes.

A trail of warmth pooled along the path.

When he spoke, I was sure I hadn't heard him right.

"What?" I asked, downplaying the reason for the huskiness in my voice. The drugs must be kicking in.

"I said I will—for a kiss."

"You'll quit. If I let you kiss me, you'll quit smoking?"

He took the pack from his pocket and held them up. "Cold turkey."

"Fine."

The wrapper crackled as he crumpled the entire pack. Without breaking my gaze, he tossed them into the kitchen trash.

I lifted my face for a peck. I should have known better. His fingers threaded beneath my jaw and into my loose hair. A hungry lust blazed in his eyes. I'd given him permission and he wasn't about to waste the shot. From beneath his hooded lids, I read promises and needs.

My eyes dropped closed. This wasn't a promise, just a kiss.

His lips were warm and soft. They feathered across mine and I meant to pull back, but his fingers held me captive. He tilted my head to the left and his tongue swept across my lips. I moaned.

I didn't mean to, it just erupted from me. His thumbs stroked my cheeks. He tasted like spearmint and, okay, a little bit of cigarette, but it wasn't grossing me out like I wanted it to. His tongue pressed against my lips again, asking. I relented and parted mine. His tongue swept into my mouth, softly probing, teasing, asking mine to dance.

Always asking. Never taking.

My hands ended up in his hair somehow and the couch dipped as he settled his knee against my hip. I leaned back until the arm of the couch dug into my shoulder blade. I wanted more of him. I moaned again and he deepened the kiss. One hand trailed down my neck to my shoulder, leaving another searing trail of heat. My body was an entire map of hotspots. These drugs must be helping.

Drugs.

I sat up fast, cracking my forehead against his chin. "Sorry."

He pressed a tender kiss against my lips. "I've never been more excited to quit smoking in my whole life."

Hair curtained his left eye, but did nothing to conceal the lust. Swelling made his lower lip droop in a sexy curve. Clearly I'd had too many drugs today.

His fingertips brushed my cheek and tucked a wayward lock behind my ear. My neck tingled. I lifted my fingers to his chest. Hard ridges of muscle jumped at my touch and his eyes flashed to my lips. I pushed him back.

Kerri cleared her throat. "Um, you guys want me to start the movie?"

She stood wide-eyed at the counter, two bowls of popcorn in her hands. She'd obviously seen the kiss, and why did I care, it was just a kiss. Something I'd done with lots of guys, just never ones I swore I wasn't going to date, and not a single musician since I'd come to college.

I nodded.

My leg ached.

My head was going to if I thought about how my heart was still thumping. I shouldn't have had a reaction if it was just a kiss.

He settled back on the couch and trapped my fingers against his chest. His heart beat strong, mocking my racing pulse. He traced each one, sending another ripple of not-lust-only-drugs thrumming through my nerves.

Still looking at Kerri, I tugged my hand away. "Start it."

She nodded and set the popcorn on the table and reclaimed her spot. I ignored her attempts at eye contact. We weren't talking about this.

Ever.

I'm not sure what I'd been thinking. I guess I thought it would be like when Axel kisses me—and clearly that had taken a wrong turn too—maybe more like when I kiss him. Brotherly, platonic, not a single urge to do it again.

By the way my lips tingled, none of those were even close to accurate.

Jesse grabbed a bowl and settled it on my stomach, then grabbed a handful, making the bowl wiggle. What should have been a calm night with friends now had a strange tilt to it because I couldn't keep my mouth shut and had to offer up something I'd clearly been wanting anyway.

A small circle of pain radiated outward from beneath my left eye. "Kerri, can I have more drugs."

She twisted and checked the kitchen clock. "Not for another forty-five minutes."

"Here," Jesse shifted on the couch, still settled against the hollow of my waist. "Give me your hand."

I lifted an eyebrow. Another ploy?

He bounced his open palm once. "Trust me. I'll do some acupressure."

"No more kissing." I settled my hand into his warm one.

"Not a sex-crazed maniac. It was just a kiss, Sasha. Not even that, just a reward."

With a gentle touch, he turned my hand over and probed the soft pad of my thumb. "Headache or leg?"

I leaned my cheek against the cushion. "Both."

"Head first then, it's faster." Squeezing the web between my thumb and index finger, he massaged a painful knot away. It hurt and felt good at the same time. After the knot melted, he gently rubbed back and forth over the spot, soothing the redness. Then he massaged each finger, pinching the tips of my fingers. "Still have a headache?"

I probed my cheek. "No. Wow, thank you. Do my leg."

"Demanding."

I smiled. "Hey. You offered."

"I did." He lowered my hand to my chest and stood. "Let me resituate first though. This one takes longer and I don't want to miss the movie."

Settled back under my legs, he drew my hand against his chest. Cradling it, he poked and massaged different points. The ache in my leg eased. When I told him, he nodded, but didn't stop. "The bone is still broken. I'm working on that now."

"You can fix her broken bone?" Kerri asked.

He shrugged. "Not instantly, but yeah, I can activate certain areas that will help it heal faster.

A few times, I thought he activated spots directly north of my legs, but when I jerked my attention off the screen, he was still watching the movie, face impassive. After my entire body felt like jelly, he lowered my hand and switched to drawing circles on my good knee. I didn't want to know it wasn't related to mending my bone, so I let him.

Jesse swirled his fingertips around my kneecap. More tingling erupted in my belly and spread outward. I reminded my body that he was a musician—a talented one who wasn't going to give it up, no matter what I said.

My body didn't care.

I picked my thumb cuticle until it bled, then switched hands. Jesse covered them with his and squeezed. His other hand quieted on my leg.

Damn, now he probably thinks it's his caresses making me destroy my fingers. Never mind that it was true, I didn't need him thinking that.

"Watch the movie, Sasha," he whispered. "Stop thinking about it."

I forced Meg Ryan's face into focus. "I am watching."

He squeezed both hands gently. "You didn't laugh at the funniest part."

Warmth crept up my neck.

"The drugs are messing with me." *Not you. Not how nice you are. Not a single thing about you bringing over pizza and a movie to make Kerri and me feel better. You're a player. You do groupies.*

He smiled and turned back to the television. "I don't always do groupies."

I jerked. No way had I said that out loud.

Kerri huffed. "You're not very nice tonight, Sasha. Jesse's been nothing but kind."

"I didn't mean—"

"It's okay." He scooted out from under my legs. "You should get some rest. Are you sleeping out here, or do you want me to help you to your room."

My eyes burned. I didn't want to admit if it was because of embarrassment, or frustration, or humiliation, so I settled on tired. I craned my neck back to meet his eyes for the first time since he kissed me. They weren't quite as shiny. I'd hurt him with my comment—unless this was more of his getting-groupies act. But I didn't think so. He'd been nothing but sincere tonight—even when he'd played me for the kiss.

One I'd wanted anyway.

I lifted my arms. "I'm ready for bed. Will you hand me my crutches and help me—"

He surged toward the couch and slid his hands gently beneath my knees and shoulders. Scooping me up, he turned. "Which way?"

Kerri beamed. Clearly in her world, touching equaled making up. By the grip Jesse had on my legs, I think it was a similar equation in his. "Last door on the right."

"Knock, knock." Axel rapped on the door.

CHAPTER 4

I stiffened.

"Stay or go?" Jesse murmured against my ear.

Kerri mouthed, "What should I do?"

I sighed. "I need to face him sometime."

"You need rest," Jesse said in his best do-me voice.
The low timbre thrummed from his chest to mine.

What I needed was some time without Jesse
touching me so I could figure out why my heart sped
up when his breath tickled my ear.

Axel knocked again.

"Hang on!" I yelled, committing me. I looked at Kerri
and jerked my head toward the door. "Go ahead."

Her gaze flickered to Jesse's.

"Help me get my crutches." I wiggled to get down
but Jesse held fast.

Kerri opened the door and Axel rushed in, then
jerked to a stop. "Oh." He glanced from Jesse to Kerri
and back to me. "I thought you were here by yourself
tonight." Flowers drooped from his hand, limp at his
side.

Jesse shifted me in his arms. "Hey, Axel."

Axel's shoulders stiffened and his chest puffed. What the hell was that? In all the time we'd spent together, he'd never, ever brought me flowers. Not even as a joke. I knew that kiss was going to screw everything up. I should have stayed last night and talked to him about it—set him firmly back in the friend zone.

While I mentally flogged myself, he apparently had time to collect himself. "Hey, Jesse. Trey said you were with her when she broke it."

I wiggled again and levered my legs against his arms. "Put me down," I hissed.

"Yeah. We went for a morning run."

Oh. My. God. Why was he making it sound like it was a post-hookup run?

Kerri shook herself out of her stupor and grabbed my crutches. She jammed one under my armpit and stared at Jesse. "I think she's fine."

He was still staring at Axel in some testosterone-fueled stand-off. Apparently, Head-of-Sasha's-Friend-Zone was quite the title. Because that's where they were both staying. Forever.

Jesse finally broke the gaze-a-thon and looked at me. I didn't like his stare any more than Axel had. Thanks to the same simmering intent beneath it. He'd claimed me.

"Please put me down," I whispered. I didn't like how helpless and pleading it sounded.

His lips parted, then closed. A muscle in his jaw bulged. He lowered me, holding me until I got my weight on my good foot. His fingertips brushed the curve of my breast and a flood of warmth raced straight to my nipples. I jerked and wobbled, but that only made his arms tighten around my back and my nipples pucker. *I have got to stop taking these drugs.*

Kerri eased between us, propping the other crutch under my arm. I sagged against her, suddenly exhausted. Jesse traded spots so he could keep his fingers beneath my arm. I tried to shrug him off. "I'm fine."

"No you're not," Axel said, clutching my other arm. Did everyone need to be touching me? "You're green."

The room tilted and I gripped the spongy handles of the crutches. "I'm good. Let's go outside."

I took a deep breath and another. The room quit acting like a sailboat in a monsoon. The three of them escorted me to the door, like they were afraid if they didn't, the other two would leap ahead in the Sasha Olympics. Ever helpful.

Kerri held my elbow and managed to open the door. Axel tossed the flowers on the counter as we went by without losing his grip on my other arm, and Jesse rubbed his hand up and down my back.

At the door, I stopped. "Okay, quit. Kerri, I'm good for a minute out here with Axel." I turned. "Jesse, go home."

He looked like I'd slapped him. I couldn't soothe his worries right now. I needed to deal with Axel and wanted more drugs and the sweet oblivion of sleep. Energy flowed out of me like a pitcher with a giant hole in the bottom. I'd be lucky if I made it through a whole conversation with Axel.

Jesse must have seen it, because he didn't argue. He got his features back under control and leaned in to kiss my cheek. "Call me if you need me," he whispered, sending my heart fluttering again, whether I had the energy or not.

I forced myself to keep calm and we made eye contact. Bright lust burned beneath his concern. "Thank you for tonight. For doing that for Kerri. She needed it," I told him.

He jerked, and the hurt surged into his features again. He opened his mouth, then clamped it shut again and nodded. "You're welcome."

Kerri hovered at the door. He leaned over and ruffled her hair. "Call me."

She smiled. "What Sasha said. Thank you."

He grinned and bounded down the stairs. I stared after him and hobbled onto the patio. Even though he told us this bad boy thing was an act, I wouldn't have believed it had I not seen that entire gamut of emotions. Maybe he wasn't quite what I thought he was.

But he was still a musician.

Axel's grip tightened on my elbow, drawing me back to the current ugly task. I nodded at Kerri and she closed the door.

I hop-crutched my way to our wicker seating area and wobbled to a stop. Axel helped me sit, and then waffled on taking the spot next to me or the opposite chair. "Just sit, Axel." My tone set the energy for this conversation. I was, apparently, going to be short and pretty blunt. Not how I wanted to do this. No matter what had happened, he was still one of my best friends. And I wanted him to be one tomorrow.

"I'm sorry," he started.

I held up my hand. "Hang tight." I eased my hips into the corner and propped my cast on the cushion. A wave of pain swept over me and I closed my eyes.

Axel lurched out of his chair and kneeled beside me. "What can I get you?"

Clutching his shoulder, I forced the patio to stop bobbing in the tsunami of pain. "Give me a sec."

"I should have been there."

"No one should have been there." The pain ebbed and I eased my fingers out of his muscles. "I fell. My foot broke, no biggie."

"Forgive me?" He slipped an arm behind me and laid his head against my stomach.

Exhaustion gripped me again and my head lolled against the hard wicker back. My hands lowered to his head and my fingers threaded through his hair.

"We can't be more than friends, you know that Axel."

"I didn't mean for it to happen, Sasha. But I don't regret it. I've wanted—"

"Shh. Please. Can we just forget it happened?"

His fingers stroked my hip. Apparently my drugs had worn off enough that I wasn't a lust-ridden maniac anymore because his touch didn't incite a swirling tide pool of heat.

He lifted his head and searched my face. "I don't want to do anything to hurt you. And if being your friend lets me hold you and hang out with you, I'll settle for it. For now."

I cradled his face between my hands. Stubble scratched my palms. "For always. You mean too much to me."

Sadness drew the corners of his mouth down, but he forced a smile. "You need sleep. Can I carry you in?"

Kerri opened the door. "Sash, you can have more drugs."

"Oh, I love you."

She glowed beneath my drunken exclamation.

I swiveled my attention to Axel. "Yes, please."

He started, then realized I was answering his question. Bending, he grabbed my crutches and handed them to Kerri, then scooped me up.

My hands were too tired to reach around his neck, so I folded them in my lap and leaned my head against his shoulder. He angled me through the door and down the hall. Kerri pulled back my covers and propped my crutches against the nightstand. She'd already plugged my phone in and settled it next to my pillow. She handed me two pills and held a glass of water. I drained both. They tucked me in and took turns kissing my forehead. I felt like I was six.

Axel closed the door and I think he started grilling Kerri about Jesse the moment darkness submerged my little boat of pain. The drugs kicked in almost immediately, or maybe my bed was just amplifying the exhaustion. Either way, I felt good for the first time all day.

My phone chirped and I fumbled around for it. Jesse texted me. *GN. Hope everything went ok with your talk. See you tomorrow?*

I closed my eyes. If I texted him back, he'd know the chat with Axel didn't take long, and I wasn't sure how I wanted him to feel about that relationship. Which should have bothered me. If Jesse and I were going to stay friends, how I behaved with my other friends should have zero bearing on whatever we had going on. But still, something made me hesitate. Probably my groovy drugs.

Sleep claimed me.

CHAPTER 5

No matter how many times I hit the shark on the head, he wouldn't let go. Blood swirled through the water. I screamed.

"Sasha!" Kerri leaned over me, shaking my shoulders. "It was a dream."

I gasped for breath and couldn't quit shaking. Kerri leaned back, hands still on my shoulders. "Are you okay? I brought you more pain medicine, but when I came in you screamed and you were thrashing around."

I wiped my eyes. My leg hurt. Bad.

Kerri tugged at the covers tangled around my leg.

I screamed. "Stop. Stop." I panted again. "It hurts bad today."

She held the glass and pills out. "Take these. I'll see if I can get you untangled."

I swallowed the pills and the water. My throat barely worked. I set the glass on the nightstand and sank into the pillow, throwing my arm over my eyes. Kerri untucked the sheet and carefully eased it off my cast.

I peered at Kerri from under my elbow. "When did Axel leave last night?"

She busied herself with the sheet. A blush colored her cheeks.

"Kerri!"

"About a half-hour ago. I crashed on the couch after you went to bed."

My arm dropped back over my eyes. "You go, girl!"

"I think he was upset about you, and I'm obviously rebounding on Trey. And we finished all Jesse's beer and some of your wine."

I laughed. "Good for you." I meant it.

She finally got my cast out of the sheet and crawled up on the bed next to me, folding one of my pillows and resting her chin on her arms. "He's a really good kisser."

"Mmm. Yeah, I know, remember."

She flicked my arm. "He really likes you."

I eased my cast across the mattress and rolled over. Her lips were swollen from their all-night make-out-fest. "And I really like him. As a friend." I grinned. "Which is a good thing if you were macking on him all night."

She blushed again. "Sorry about that."

"I'm not. He's a super-nice guy. I think he's a perfect rebound for you." I plucked one of her sleepy curls and tugged it. "Except it's going to be my shoulder he's crying on when you crush him."

She winked. "Perfect. Then you can be his rebound."

I grimaced.

"Speaking of Jesse—"

"We weren't."

"Yeah, nice try avoiding me on that one. What happened to the 'no musician rule?'"

"It's still firmly in place, trust me," I reassured her.

"Uh-huh. So the kiss?"

"Merely taking one for the team. I got him to quit smoking."

"Right." She poked me in the side. "That's all it was."

I looked away.

"Did you like it?"

Did I? Without thinking, my hands traced my lower lip and I stared at the ceiling. I'd kissed my fair share of guys, but that kiss had been laced with something deeper, something that tugged at parts of me I didn't really want to think about this early in the morning.

Kerri giggled. "You totally did."

"Maybe."

She sat up. "I knew it! I knew you'd like him if you just gave him a chance. Plus he's super hot."

"Until he quits singing, none of that matters."

"Maybe he's different."

I sat up. My tee was completely twisted around my waist. I straightened it and tugged it down. "He's not, Kerri. They never are."

She scooted off the bed and supported my arm until I got balanced on my good foot. I had to hop a few times, but got my crutches situated. "I'm starving."

"You really won't give him a shot?"

"He's obviously a nice guy, and I'm fine being friends." I scowled. "But that's it."

She sighed. "I think you're missing out."

I shrugged. "Maybe."

She wrinkled her nose at me, and I hoped she was going to leave it. "I haven't gone grocery shopping yet. You think you can make it to the car?"

I was still in yesterday's running gear and I hadn't showered, but I wasn't exactly sure I was ready to tackle water and plastic bags. Kerri hadn't gotten dressed either, and if we went to Jinnie's we'd be surrounded by the pajama-wearing, hangover crowd.

My stomach rumbled again. "I need to figure it out eventually. Give me a sec to redo my pony and pee, then we'll go."

She leaned over my dresser and ran her fingers through her hair. "Okay. Me too."

The bathroom proved easier than I thought and my hair wasn't a complete gooey mess yet. Maybe tonight I could try the shower or a bath. I dragged a brush through my tangles.

"Will you stay over tonight? I think I want to try a shower tonight," I told Kerri, wanting her to know I needed her and wasn't just looking out for her while she got over Trey. I wobbled out of the bathroom and Kerri went in. "I'm going to head to the car." I figured I'd need the head start.

"I'll only be a sec. Be careful."

I was slowly getting the hang of the crutches. The stairs made me a little nervous though. I think there was a way to do it, but couldn't remember if I put my foot first, or the crutches. I managed the door okay, but paused on the top step.

Kerri tugged the door behind her and raced down the steps. She turned and held up both hands, ready to catch me if I botched this. "Crutches first."

I lowered them to the first step, then hopped down. Before I wobbled out of control, I repeated the pattern and took a deep breath when all my parts were upright on the sidewalk. She opened the car door and I handed her my crutches, then eased in. *Okay, this wasn't so bad*. I relaxed into the seat and Kerri wedged my crutches along the door.

After she got in, we stared at each other and laughed. "We're a mess."

"I know, right?" I reached across and grabbed her hand. "I don't know what I'd do without you, Ker."

She lifted the back of my hand to her cheek. "Me either. Boys are dumb, but I'll always have you."

"Always."

Lowering my hand, she started the car. "Where to?"

"I was thinking Jinnie's."

"Ooh, perfect. Omelets."

The wait wasn't too bad, especially for a Sunday morning. A group of guys gave up their seats in the waiting area for us and normally I'd have waved it off, but I was still tired. And my leg still hurt.

"How long before this thing heals?" I asked her, not remembering any of the instructions the doctor had given me.

"At least six weeks."

I scrunched up my face. "Not cool."

"Hey." One of the boys who'd given up his seat jerked his chin toward my cast. "You don't have a single rugby player signature on that."

I laughed. He was cute. Gigantic, but cute. "No. This is a rugby-free zone."

His face fell and a few of the other guys turned to listen. "What if I can get you the entire team?"

One of his buddies was eyeing Kerri. I wasn't sure a rugby player was any better than a frat boy, but they were insanely fit, which might make for a fun play toy. Kerri flirted back. It was just a cast.

I tipped it left and right. "I'm not sure there's enough room."

He swiped the screen of his phone. "One call and I can have them all here."

His smile was charming, and obviously the playful sort.

This was so silly. And I couldn't stop smiling.

The hostess called his group and the Kerri admirer typed her number into his phone. "I'll call you."

Another group of hangovers arrived, crowding the small space. He needed to get to his table, but stood his ground while people flowed around him—and my cast as he stood there protecting it. I grinned up at him. "Do it."

"Don't leave before they get here."

I laughed and drew an 'X' over my heart. "Promise."

He held out a hand. "I'm Dew."

I cocked my head and reached out to shake his hand. "Really?"

He lifted my fingers to his lips. "Short for Dwight."

"Sasha." Charming as Dew might be, nothing tingled when he released my fingers. I wanted to be attracted to him. I smiled through the confusion. His full lips turned up and his green eyes twinkled with mischief.

"A pleasure, Sasha."

Our table was ready, and I was kind of glad the hostess lead us to the other side of the restaurant. Dew was hot, but my lack of response wasn't cool. Plus I was super-starving, which meant I was about to inhale a ridiculous amount of food and didn't need the rugby team cheering me on.

Jinnie's omelets were legendary, and since I wasn't going to get any running in anytime soon, I'd get to enjoy my fair share over the next month.

We slid into the booth and I stashed my trip sticks under the table. I was finally getting the hang of them and didn't feel like I was going to crash into everything. I tossed my phone on the table next to Kerri's and we ordered coffee. Settling back with my menu, I flipped the page. Jinnie's boasted an awe inspiring selection of omelets and sometimes it was nearly overwhelming.

Kerri sat up and wrapped on the window, then waved. I looked up from my menu and jerked, then slid down in the seat. Maybe Jesse wouldn't see me. His black hoodie swiveled toward me and he pierced me with his stare, then one side of his mouth curved up. He drummed his fingers against the glass, pointed to his own chest, then our table.

Kerri nodded and waved him in.

"Kerri," I hissed as he jogged toward the front door.

"What? It's just breakfast with friends." Her smirk said otherwise.

"Knock it off."

She held up her menu, shielding her face. "No idea what you're talking about."

The waitress brought our coffee and waters. Jesse planted a hand around her waist to keep her from ramming into him. She smiled and batted her eyelashes. I gagged. Was anyone not affected by his oversexed charm?

"Can I get the same?" He waved his hand over our cups.

She touched his arm. "Of course."

I didn't scoot over. If Kerri wanted him, he could sit over there.

He stretched his arm across the back of my seat and tucked his hips against mine. "Hey baby."

I still didn't scoot. Maybe if half his butt was hanging off the bench he'd get the hint.

His eyes dropped to my shoulders and he lowered his face to my neck.

I lurched sideways. "What the hell?"

He sifted his fingers through my hair. "What's wrong?"

I pressed my hand against his chest and bounced to the edge of the booth. "You. Kissing me. Your no-smoking reward changed nothing."

"That's not what you told me last night."

I scowled. "What are you talking about?"

His face fell, then lit up and he laughed. "Were you drunk texting me?"

My mouth opened and Kerri and I reached for my phone at the same time. She snatched it and I wrestled it from her.

She'd already gotten into the message. As I scanned the words, not a single recollection came back to me. Drugged texting was a thousand times worse than drunk texting. Warmth flooded my face. They got worse.

The only one I remembered was his first: *GN. Hope everything went ok with your talk. See you tomorrow?*

From there, I drew a blank.

Thanks. You were sweet to come over.

I like hanging with you.

Me too. The kissing part was great. We should do that more.

I slapped my phone face down on the table. Kerri slipped it from beneath my fingers and scrolled through the conversation. She did a pretty good job of keeping her excitement in check. I didn't dare look at Jesse.

The waitress showed up with Jesse's coffee. "We ready to order?"

I shoved my face in my menu while Kerri and Jesse ordered. "The Avocadonado, please." She took our menus and smiled at Jesse again. Bold flirting with a guy bookended by two chicks. He was such a musician. Groupies could smell him a mile away.

Kerri slid my phone back. Jesse intercepted it and scrolled to the bottom. "So I guess you didn't mean any of this?"

"I do like hanging with you."

He twirled the phone between his index fingers and thumb, like an intoxicated pinwheel. "But not kissing me?"

Kerri squirmed like someone had flipped the switch on her seat heater, but—impressively—she kept her mouth shut.

"It wasn't a kiss, it was to make you quit smoking."

"Then if that wasn't a kiss, there's no reason we can't keep doing it. I feel like smoking right now."

I huffed and crossed my arms. "Have a sucker."

"How about a kiss?"

"You can't have a kiss every time you have a craving. It was a one-time deal."

"Fine, then I'll go smoke."

Silence stretched and I waited for him to get up. What did I care if he killed himself in a long, slow death from cancer?

"Sasha?"

I didn't look at him. I was having a hard enough time ignoring the lust pounding at my throat, if I looked at him, all my resolve would vanish.

He leaned his shoulder into mine. "I was kidding. I won't kiss you if you didn't like it."

I couldn't say that with a straight face, but we weren't ever going to do it again so it didn't matter whether I'd liked it or not. Blanking my face so I didn't reveal a thing, I smiled and met his eyes. "I like where we're at."

He nodded once. "Then that's where we'll stay."

I didn't believe him, but it was enough to get me through breakfast—which luckily arrived before I had to say anything. He looked down his nose at mine while drizzling syrup over his full stack. Without comment, he handed me the bottle. I poured a pool in the corner of my plate.

He coughed. "You're not serious."

"Shut it."

I cut a corner of the avocado explosion that may have contained eggs and dipped it in the syrup. "How fast today?"

Pancakes paused at his lips. "Nine."

"How far?"

"Seven."

"I hate you."

"Run with me when you're foot's healed and I'll get you there." He popped the pancakes in.

"You'll be a great trainer." Kerri waved her fork in the air. "Just pretend you're going to kiss her."

My face heated up and I hid behind my coffee mug.

Jesse laughed and high-fived Kerri. Jerks.

Breakfast wasn't horrible. Again. He was making a habit out of being charming. Good thing we were just friends.

A commotion on the far side of the restaurant saved me from any further humiliation.

"Oh my." Kerri's exclamation lifted my head. I swallowed quickly to keep from spewing coffee over the table. Dew and a herd of fit, barely dressed men were headed toward our table—not a boy among them. Sculpted muscle bunched and flexed beneath cut-off sweatshirts, tank tops, and jerseys. My eyes bulged and I swallowed as they jostled and bumped against each other, moving like a pack of wild hyenas. Dew moved with a purposeful stride and I squirmed, feeling very pursued.

A few feet from the table, he grinned and jerked his thumb over his shoulder. "Told you."

I grinned. "So you did."

Kerri leaned across the table and shoved Jesse. "Move. They're going to sign her cast."

Jesse looked at me, then Dew, and then surveyed the entire rugby team. "Hey guys."

Dew leaned forward and bumped Jesse's knuckles. "You sounded great last week, man."

"Thanks. You guys taking the Conference this year?" Jesse stood and took a step back, leaning an elbow against the neighboring booth.

Dew pulled a sharpie from his front pocket. "That's the plan."

Jesse nodded. "Right on."

I eased my leg onto the bench and scooted toward the end to give Dew and the team plenty of space to spread their muscles—and signatures.

Dew tapped Jesse's inscription with his index finger, making my leg wiggle, then gave Jesse a sideways glance. I didn't have to look at Jesse to know his chest just puffed an entire shirt size. Dew answered in kind.

Fantastic, a peacock strutting contest, right here over my omelet.

Dew wasn't as overt, choosing only to scribe his name and rugby number. I glanced up long enough to catch Jesse's glare, then down to my cast. I blinked. Okay, maybe Dew wasn't as subtle as I thought—he'd added his phone number too.

He handed the sharpie to the next player in line and I was the intense scrutiny of fifteen of the dreamiest—*gawd, was that even still a word?*—fit bodies I'd ever been that close to. My cast looked like a kid's autographed rugby ball by the time they finished. Dew pushed back through the crowd and tapped the tabletop with the tip of his marker. "Don't be shy about using that number. We practice every afternoon, but otherwise, I'm around."

I stared up at him—looking like a complete idiot, I'm sure—and nodded. "I will."

The player who'd been flirting up Kerri winked at her and she ducked her head. Good grief, we were acting like complete groupies.

They left and I could almost feel Jesse bristling and gnashing over my shoulder. What was his problem? I'd been super clear from the beginning that we weren't going anywhere. There was absolutely nothing wrong with me crushing on a hardbody.

He moved to the end of the table and I looked up from my cast. He scowled at my fingers resting on Dew's number and opened his mouth, then shut it again. The muscle in his jaw clenched.

I notched my chin higher.

His gaze lingered on my lips, then lifted. I arched an eyebrow, daring him to comment. Instead of taking the challenge, he drummed the tabletop and turned. "Catch you later."

He stopped the waitress and said something. She turned up the wattage of her smile, then glanced at our table and nodded. He pulled a bill from his wallet and handed it to her. I think she tried to give him change, but he shook his head, then left.

Kerri cleared her throat. "Well, that was awkward."

I straightened and swung my cast to the floor. "It shouldn't be—or wouldn't be–if he'd bother to listen."

"You can't blame him, Sash." Kerri pushed her plate back. "Especially after—"

"Do. Not." I didn't even remotely want to revisit the texts.

She huffed. "Well, it's true."

"Texting under the influence gets an automatic pass."

She scrunched her nose.

"Please," I stabbed my last forkful of egg. "If you had to answer for every one of your drunk texts . . ."

"Alright, alright." She laughed.

"That rugby boy is super cute."

Her eyes widened. "Which one?"

We laughed.

CHAPTER 6

Back at the house, Kerri curled up with her geography notes and I worked on conjugating French verbs until my eyes blurred. Clouds obscured the sky and a light rain ushered in the afternoon. When I couldn't keep my eyes open I tossed my notes on the coffee table and eased myself upright. A cool breeze drifted through the room and I hobbled to the front door. Jesse's silhouette at the end of the walk didn't surprise me. I pushed through the screen door and hopped onto the porch.

Arms deep in the front pocket of his sweatshirt, Jesse lifted his head. My heart lurched at the forlorn edge to his features. I wanted us to be friends, not this, whatever it was.

"Out for a run?" I yelled through the drizzle.

He didn't answer.

The wind picked up and a gust slipped around the side of the porch, knocking me off balance. I scrambled for a handhold, but the bench was too far away. My weight shifted and I pinwheeled my arms. Solid arms wrapped around my waist and held me over the warped boards of our aging patio. I pressed my palms into them until they shook. My hamstring burned with trying to keep my cast from hitting.

Jesse slid his arms further around me and squatted until he held my full weight. Was I ever going to stop leaning on him? I exhaled and my body trembled. Another gust buffeted us and he lost his balance. I shrieked and braced myself for the jolt of pain. His arms tightened around me and he twisted, landing on his back and breaking my fall. My chest smashed into his and my chin dug into his sternum.

He groaned, but his arms held me tight.

I twisted. Somehow, he'd managed to catch my cast with his ankle and had his foot propped against the bench. Relief flooded my limbs and I sagged against him. He bent his knee so our legs weren't angled so awkwardly.

His cellphone dug into my stomach and I inched higher, not feeling stable enough to stand just yet. I squeezed my eyes closed and willed the patio to stop spinning. These pain meds were going to be the death of me. My skin tingled where Jesse's fingers rested on the base of my skull and the small of my back.

"If you keep fidgeting like that, I'm going to need a cigarette."

I froze.

He chuckled and the sensation vibrated through my torso.

"You said you quit."

He cleared his throat. "Yeah well, now I need one for an entirely different reason."

Suddenly very aware of his body beneath mine and my breasts rubbing against his chest, I tugged my hands from between our bodies and pushed. His grip tightened and his fingers traced small circles across my skin. As much as I wanted to hate his touch, it made me feel safe, and tingly.

I opened my eyes and stared at the crooked porch railing. It rolled and swayed like the deck of a boat. I closed my eyes again. Maybe it wouldn't hurt to lie here for another minute until I got my bearings.

Wind lifted sections of hair and brushed them across my face. Jesse combed them back and tucked them behind my ear. More tingling waves radiated outward from his fingers along my skin.

"How many cigarettes have you had?"

"Since the deal?"

I nodded, grinding my cheek against the soft nap of his sweatshirt.

"None."

I lifted my head and rested my chin against his chest, raising one eyebrow.

His fingers trailed down my neck and rested on my shoulder. "I'm serious."

He did look honest. And I couldn't smell it on him. But he was chewing that green gum again.

"And I'm supposed to just believe you?"

The corner of his mouth turned up. "Never. You should always do a taste test."

I rolled my eyes and lay my head back down. Even with his teasing, he felt good. And solid.

He lifted his hand and let my hair sift through his fingers. I'd taken it out of the ponytail several French verbs ago when my headache made an energetic return. I still hadn't taken a shower and it was freaking me out a little that he was so contentedly playing with it. And that I was so contentedly letting him.

"Sasha!" Kerri's alarmed scream made me jerk upright, elbowing Jesse in the gut.

He groaned and curled inward, rolling us over.

Kerri raced through the door, slamming the screen door into Jesse's ankle.

"Damn! You girls are going to kill me."

I eased up on my hands and knees. Jesse pulled up in a crouch and helped me stand. Kerri wedged her hands over the top of his and together they helped me into the house.

"I'm fine." Jesse supported most of my weight and Kerri pulled the door shut behind us.

"I looked up and you were gone. Then I remembered hearing a thud. God, Sash, I'm so sorry."

I laughed. "Yeah, fat lot of help you are."

"Good thing Jesse's always around at the right time."

My heart sped up. *Yeah, good thing.*

He eased me onto the couch and settled next to me. "I didn't bring dinner this time."

Kerri's gaze bounced to Jesse's arm around my shoulders to my hand resting on his thigh. I moved it, but she scrambled toward her purse. "I'll go. Chinese okay?"

Jesse tucked me tighter against his side. Exhaustion tugged at my limbs and I nodded at Kerri.

She raced out the door. "Be back in five."

Jesse tucked my head into his chest and his magic fingers started again at my nape. A moan-sigh noise trickled from my lips. As badly as I wanted to blame my response on the drugs, I couldn't remember taking any since this morning. Which meant my earlier dizziness wasn't from them either.

His thumb pressed into the tight cord in my neck and pain jolted down my arm. I moaned.

"Does that hurt?"

"Yes, but the good kind."

I think his lips pressed against my temple, but his fingers dug into the knot next to my spine and I couldn't concentrate on anything else. He hit another sore spot and I gasped. My fingers dug into his thigh.

"Should I stop?" His voice sounded husky.

"Mmm." I couldn't manage anything more. Colors swirled behind my closed eyes. A tingle radiated outward from my toes and up both my shins. My body sagged against him and he shifted me until I was resting on my stomach across his thighs. His fingers squeezed and pressed against my tight muscles until the knots released one by one. Sliding down my spine, his fingers worked over every bump in my spine and fiber of muscle. The hem of my t-shirt inched upward and his fingertips brushed my skin. A burst of fireworks erupted in my belly and I fought the urge to press upward into his hand. I squeezed my eyes shut and his hand moved upward over the fabric again.

I sighed.

"Better?"

Part of me wanted to say yes, but the other half didn't want him to quit. "If I say yes, will you stop?" My words sounded slurred with my lips pressed into the couch.

He chuckled and shifted. "Here. Sit up and turn."

I rose, awkwardly bumping against his chest and the back of the couch. He slipped his hands beneath my arms and turned us both until his back rested against the arm and our legs extended across the entire couch. The couch dipped and my butt settled against him. I swallowed, but before I could move away, he cupped my shoulders and dug into those muscles. All awkwardness fled and I relaxed.

He worked his way across different angles of my neck and back to my shoulders, following the muscles and tendons to the front. At the collar of my shirt, he hesitated, then retreated back to my shoulders. He bent his knee and I sank deeper into the sagging couch. My hands gripped the middle of his thighs, and I unclenched my fingers.

He laughed. "Thanks. That's some grip."

I rubbed them briskly, then froze when he stiffened. At least he'd changed into running pants and I wasn't touching his bare skin.

His fingers slid across the neck of my shirt and I bit my lip. He worked the top of my chest muscle—no differently than any other massage—but my heart hadn't ever sped up like this. The pressure eased, and his touch became a caress across my skin. I arched my back and his fingers dipped lower over the curve of my breast, stretching the neck of my shirt. Warm breath tickled my hair and his lips pressed against my ear. My palms flattened against his thighs and I rubbed them in slow circles. He leaned us back. Trading the neck of my shirt for the hem, he slid his hand across my stomach, making my skin jump. His tongue traced the edge of my ear and I tipped my face, granting him access to my neck. As his hands slid higher and cupped my breasts, I arched my back and the curve of my ass rubbed against him.

He froze. My hands stilled on his thigh. I could feel his heart pounding against my back and his heavy breathing lifted me up and down. Slowly, he pulled his hand from under my shirt and pressed his forehead against my ear.

"I can't be just friends, Sasha." He sat up and tucked his fingers beneath my hips, then eased me a few inches away. "This was a bad idea."

Was it? Two days ago I'd been certain about how I felt. Now I wasn't so sure. His thighs were rock hard beneath my fingers. I should move, but something inside knew if I did there'd be no going back. I'd forever seal him into the Friend Zone.

That's what I wanted, right?

My hard lines were beginning to blur. *Maybe he really is different.*

I stiffened and lifted my hands into my own lap. No.

Easing my way over his thighs, I scooted to the far side of the couch. When I met his eyes, I flinched. He saw the exit sign to the Friend Zone too.

It's the only way, Sasha.

"You're right. I'm sorry. If we're going to be friends, we should cool all the touching." My guts jumped at my words. A sure sign that my lines weren't just blurred—they didn't even exist anymore.

CHAPTER 7

By the time Kerri came back, Jesse had already made his awkward departure. We didn't bother making a plan of when we'd see each other next, and his tortured look haunted me all the way through the Chinese. Even Mr. Woo's secret sauce did nothing to ease my discomfort.

Kerri popped the back half of her eggroll into her mouth. "So what happened?"

"Nothing. Seriously, we were on the couch—"

"Cuddled up like a pair of mittens."

I snorted my Coke. "Mittens?"

She shrugged and stole one of my wontons. "Best I could come up with. I've never seen you cuddle like that."

Warmth crept up my neck. "We weren't cuddling."

She lifted an eyebrow and didn't even bother to respond.

"Okay. We were cuddling, but he was rubbing my shoulders."

"Mmm-hmm."

My palms still tingled. His toned legs were hot. I hadn't expected that. I don't know what I expected— clearly I'd never thought I'd be rubbing them. And based on what he was pressing into my backside, he thought some of my parts were hot too.

I glance up into Kerri's intense stare. "What . . . else . . . happened? Ohmigod. Sasha!"

My blush intensified and she raced around the counter. "You did not. Did you guys make out *again?*"

I jammed a forkful of sweet 'n sour chicken into my mouth and shook my head.

"You liar." She pushed my shoulder and jammed her fists into her hips. "Tell me."

I closed my eyes and gave my head the barest of nods.

"Why don't you torture the guy already. After you made out did you remind him of the friend thing?"

Another tiny nod.

She tossed her head back and groaned. "You're evil. Plain evil."

I swallowed. "I thought it was the drugs at first, but I haven't had any today."

She glared. "That's a shit excuse, Sasha."

I dropped my forehead to the counter. "I know."

Silence stretched between us. The clock above the fridge ticked away the seconds.

"Do you like him or are you just horny."

My silence answered for me.

"So now what?"

I rolled my head back and forth in a helpless gesture.

Kerri stroked my hair. "Want to know what I think?"

"Not really—I mean, yes."

My phone rang and I squeezed my eyes shut. But then I remembered that Jesse'd never called me. Later tonight I could expect a text.

Kerri slid my phone over and I stared at the number. It looked vaguely familiar. "Hello?"

"Sasha? Hey, it's Dew," came from the other end.

I avoided Kerri's death stare. She wasn't done talking about Jesse and deep in my belly I knew what her advice was going to be. I wasn't ready yet.

Spinning around on the stool, I cradled the phone against my shoulder. "Hi."

"Did all those signatures make your foot heal yet?"

I smiled. "Not yet." Behind me, Kerri clattered plates against each other and crammed our Styrofoam containers back in the paper bag. It wasn't possible for her to make more noise. I eased myself off the stool and hobbled toward the couch.

"That's too bad. Hey, I wanted to see if you want to come to our game tomorrow."

"I have labs until six."

"That's okay. The game doesn't start until seven."

Kerri slammed a cabinet door and I flinched.

"Okay, then I guess, yes."

"Super. Can I pick you up?"

I hadn't given much thought to how I was going to get around tomorrow. Kerri's car was going to be mandatory. No way could I get myself around, and the walk to campus was a couple blocks. Tomorrow was our worst afternoon for coordination. "Sure, but can we meet at the chem lab parking lot?"

He paused. "Uh, sure. See you tomorrow?"

"Bye." I hung up and leaned my head into the couch.

"Who was that?" Kerri jammed napkins into the trash.

"Like you don't know. Are you going to the game to watch your rugby player tomorrow?"

She shook her head. "He hasn't called."

Nice. Way to be an ass, Sash. "Oh. Well will you go with me?"

"Pretty sure Dew thinks that's a date."

"To a game? That he's playing in? Doubt it."

She pushed her stool in and leaned against the counter, keeping an entire room between us.

I sighed and closed my eyes. "Will you come over here and talk?"

Nothing moved on that side of the room.

"And bring pain medicine."

That got her moving, but made me feel like an even bigger jerk. She tossed me the bottle and I barely opened my eyes before they cracked me in the nose.

"Thanks." I swallowed the pills dry.

"Just give him a chance, Sasha."

I closed my eyes. One of the pills was lodged on the left side of my throat. "Why? Why should I be the one to break my rules?"

"Because you *like* him, for one."

"Or my drugged brain thinks he's hot."

"You know that's not true."

I squeezed my eyes and twisted my fingers in the hem of my shirt. "Which is why I need to go out with Dew more than any other reason."

Kerri huffed.

I propped myself up on my elbows. "Are you mad?"

Swinging her bag over her shoulder, she shrugged. "More disappointed, I think. Jesse is great and you're condemning him because he happens to be a super talented musician. That's not a crime, Sasha. Not for the rest of us. I'm going home."

I fell into the couch and threw my arm over my eyes. "Then you date him," I said, giving up.

"He doesn't want me." The door closed softly behind her, echoing through an empty house.

CHAPTER 8

rough classes was worse than I'd
ndays were my heaviest days, and
exception. After a botched shower
attempt, I gave up and rinsed my hair, then managed
a pair of sweats and tee. My bag was nearly
impossible to keep on and every time it slid off, I got
off balance. Add four hundred students all going the
opposite way and it was a wonder I hadn't crushed a
few kneecaps with my crutches.

By the time my chemistry lab rolled around, I was
ready to cry.

I couldn't wait to get home and crash on the couch. I
hadn't talked to Kerri all day, and Jesse didn't text
me last night either. Today, I'd been adrift alone.

Apparently everyone else had a shitty Monday too
because I had the chem lab practically to myself. I'd
done most of my work last week, so I wasn't in a
hurry to get everything finished. I had plenty of time,
even if I took the whole lab.

My phone rang and I glanced at the clock. Wow. I'd
totally lost track of time. It was after six.

"Hey, are you coming out?"

Oh! I sagged back onto my stool. I'd completely
forgotten about Dew's game. *Shit.* I lowered my

forehead to the counter. Clearly this outfit wasn't going to work if he really thought tonight was a date. If possible, I looked even worse than yesterday.

On the other end of the line, Dew yelled at someone.

"Uh, yeah. I'm just finishing up. Be right out."

"Great! We're totally amped for this game. I'm glad you'll be there when we crush them."

"Yeah." I tried to infuse some enthusiasm into my voice, but it fell flat.

Dew hung up and I groaned. My foot throbbed and I should totally be going home to put it up and reload on my meds until I passed out. I should have begged off.

Standing, I gathered my books and put away my testing rods. I had no idea how long rugby games lasted, but hopefully I could escape home by nine. My bag rammed me in the back and I shifted the contents, tossing me to the left. Maybe before the end of the week, I'd have the crutches figured out, or the genius to empty my bag. I winced and headed to the parking lot.

Dew sat in a blue Tacoma. Giant wheels and massive lift made me oh-so-eager to try climbing in. He hopped down and grabbed my bag. "Here, you're gonna need a hand."

I smiled. He smelled good and bounded around like an golden retriever. "Thanks." We rounded the back of his truck and he lifted me onto the seat, then bounded away without shutting the door. I eyed the yawning gap between the ground and the door, then twisted my hand around the seatbelt and leaned over. My cast slipped and banged against the doorframe. By now, I'd become nearly immune to the throbbing pains. I bit my lip and yanked the door shut, barely getting my cast out of the way before it slammed.

Dew fired up the truck and tore out of the parking lot, barely noticing that I'd managed to not fall out. "We beat these guys last year, but they've added a couple new freshmen. Man I hope we spank them again."

"Mmmhmm."

Dew's phone rang and he jammed it against his shoulder. "Yeah man. Almost there." He tossed the phone on the dash and glanced at me with a sideways grin. "You okay if we park by the locker rooms and you walk around to the entrance?"

Was he for real? I lifted a crutch. "Uh, not exactly."

He laughed and slapped his leg. "Oh, right."

Cutting across three lanes of traffic, he made a wide right turn. I gripped the door handle to keep from tumbling across the seat and into his lap. My foot banged up into the heater vent. This better be a short game.

He screeched to a halt and drummed his fingers on the steering wheel.

"No, I've got it." Sarcasm dripped from my words.

"Oh geez." He raced around, yanked my door, and set me down. "Come down to the locker room after, okay?"

Without waiting for a response, he bounded into the truck and tore away. I guess there were worse things than musicians.

I hobbled my way to the ticket booth, showed my student ID and eased through the gate. There weren't a lot of participants since today was a pre-season game, so I snagged a chair at the top of the main landing. I wasn't up to any more effort than was necessary.

Players took to the field and I had no idea how rugby was played, but I followed along with the crowd and tried to cheer and boo at the appropriate times. My foot throbbed, but I propped it on the empty row in front of me.

Thankfully the game ended and Dew's team did, indeed, crush the visiting team. I was ready to go. He waved from the field and I made my way down the steps and toward the locker room. My phone had been suspiciously silent during the game and I wondered what Kerri was doing. And who she was with. Monday was our make-a-plan-for-the-week night and I always stayed at Kerri's. Maybe that was aggravating the situation since I was here. I'd text her on the way home and see what she was up to.

Dew came out of the locker room freshly showered and buoyant again. I wondered if he ever chilled out completely. Six guys accompanied him and I recognized all of them from Jinnie's. They gave me good-natured smiles and elbowed Dew.

After lots of high-fiving, Dew slung an arm around my shoulders and I wobbled. "Everyone's going to Sam's. You up for a quick drink?"

I shook my head. "Not tonight. I need to get home."

His face fell. "I thought we were hanging out?"

"No. I watched the game, but my foot is killing me."

"Oh. I've got drugs in—" he jerked a thumb toward the locker room.

"It's okay. I just need to get off it."

"Sam has a couch."

He led me toward the truck, and I eased out from under his arm. "You go ahead. I'll call Kerri."

"No. I'll take you. Let me just swing by there and tell him I'll be back."

He lifted me into the truck and fished a beer bottle out from a cooler in the back. "Want one?"

"No thanks."

He shrugged and popped the top, then drove in the opposite direction of my house. I tapped out a text to Kerri. Three blocks from the stadium, he angled the truck in a driveway and hopped out. "You sure you don't want to come in and put that foot up?"

I smiled and tried my best at politeness. "No. Maybe some other time."

Kerri didn't answer right away, so I twisted on the seat and put my foot up as best as I could. The throbbing lessened a bit.

More high fiving on the patio, and Dew slipped inside. I had a bad feeling I wasn't going to see him anytime soon, but if I went in after him, I'd never get home. I checked my phone. Still nothing from Kerri. I could always try Axel. If Kerri didn't respond in the next ten minutes, I would.

And there was always Jesse. But he didn't have a car, and I wasn't about to make him carry me all ten blocks back to my house. I dug through my bag and found my meds. All Dew had was beer, and these things were bad enough on their own, I didn't need to add any alcohol. My throat was parched, but I managed to find a half-empty water bottle at the bottom of my bag. That helped.

Still nothing from Kerri.

I stared up and down the street. I was pretty sure I knew where I was, and there was no way I'd make it all the way home on my crutches—at least not with my bag.

Axel would come get me in a heartbeat, but he was still probably super clingy. *Come on, Kerri.*

I glanced at the house. Dew laughed at something one of his teammates said and filled his cup from the keg again. Even if he did ever make it back to the truck, I wasn't sure I wanted him behind the wheel.

Call me old fashioned.

I swiped my phone and got ready to call Axel.

Knuckles wrapped my window and I screeched. A familiar black hoodie stared up at me.

I rolled down the window.

"Need a lift?"

Relief flooded me. I didn't even care it was Jesse who'd come to my rescue. "Yes! Oh please."

He opened the door and slipped his hands beneath my arms and gently lowered me. "Can you stand or do I need to carry you?"

I must have hesitated too long, because he swung me up in his arms and strode to Kerri's car. "Where's Kerri?"

"Tell you in a sec." He eased me into the back and raced back to Dew's truck for the rest of my things.

Dew came out on the porch and lifted a hand. "Thanks man."

Jesse waved back. "No prob."

Boys are so lame.

Jesse stashed my crutches and bag in the back, then slipped in beside me. He leaned over to kiss my cheek, then froze and straightened. My pulse hammered and his look sucked. I didn't want to be the bad guy.

I wanted him to kiss me.

And not on the cheek.

He busied himself with starting the car and I folded my hands in my lap.

"I was at Kerri's house when you texted."

My head jerked up.

"We met at the Redbox and she seemed down. Neither one of us had anything going on tonight." He flipped the car around and eased out of the neighborhood. "I thought you'd be home too. I didn't realize she wasn't staying with you anymore."

He was silent so long, I glanced sideways to gauge his attitude. The easygoing Jesse had vanished somewhere around the last stop sign.

I struggled for something to say. "Well, I'm glad you were there."

His lips pressed together in a narrow line. "She'd been drinking, so we thought it would be better for me to come get you." He flipped the turn signal on. Tonight he was being safety sam and it was kind of freaking me out. I liked the in-your-face balls-to-the-wall Jesse. I'd come to rely on that guy for laughs. If ever a moment needed a laugh, it was this one.

"I'll take you home then take her car back."

"That's such a pain. I'm sorry."

His head jerked up. "I'm the one who should be apologizing. I'm probably bringing you down. Dew seemed happy that they won."

Ah. I could be so dense sometimes. In my defense—drugs. Surely I could blame them for this too.

"Yeah. He's very into rugby."

"I didn't realize you were."

I twisted in the seat and cupped his forearm. "I'm not."

He braked in front of my house.

"I'm not, Jesse."

Strain creased the corners of his eyes. I'd done this, and it made me feel awful. Kerri was right. I needed to give him a chance and stop making him pay for my mistakes in my past. He'd been nothing but good to me. From the very beginning. Tonight he'd gone out of his way to pick me up from what he thought was a date gone bad.

He fidgeted in his seat and a lump of awkward sat between us. "There's a big concert tomorrow night. It's basically a giant collection of rock bands." He smirked. "I know that's not your thing, but one of the bands I've idolized my whole life is coming. I thought, maybe if you heard them you'd understand why I'm so into music."

My heart twisted. There was no way to easily explain the musician thing.

"We get a couple tickets and passes for playing." His hands raced back and forth across the steering wheel. "You and Kerri should come. I can get another ticket for me somewhere else so you don't even have to sit with me."

I lay my hand on his forearm. He flinched. "Will you go with me?"

His gaze jerked to mine. "I can't go as friends, Sasha. Please don't ask me to. Take Kerri. You'll have fun. Our band will be done by four—we have the first set—you won't even have to watch us if you don't want to."

"Jesse." My voice softened and I leaned closer, slipping my fingers to his chin. I tugged gently until he looked at me. "I'm not asking you to go as friends."

He blanched, like I'd punched him, and his gaze rapidly flicked back and forth across my face. "Don't tease me, Sasha. Not today, okay?"

I wet my lips and slipped my hand behind his neck. Tugging gently, I met him more than halfway. At the first touch of our lips, he jerked like I'd electrocuted him. I pressed closer, tasting the curve of his lips.

His hands gripped my shoulders and he held me a breath away. His lips moved against mine. "What are you doing?"

I slid my other hand across his chest. He shivered. I opened my eyes and stared into his questioning ones. "Asking you to not be friends."

His fingers tightened on my shoulders. "I'm serious, Sasha. If you're going to wake up in the morning and forget this, please get out of the car."

I sighed and leaned back. "Fine."

His face twisted and I grabbed his hand.

"But I need you to come in with me." His chivalry wouldn't let me walk to the house by myself, and I was counting on being a bit more convincing when I didn't have a gearshift and armrest to maneuver over.

Before I could get my crutches and bag positioned, Jesse was around the car and helping me out. I bit back the smile. I needed to stay on my game if I was going to convince him I was being serious. His hands slid beneath my arms and I winced—only partially faking.

He took my bag and slipped it over his shoulder, then wound an arm behind my back. I moaned and leaned into him.

"Here, let me get your crutches." He shifted me so I was leaning on Kerri's car. If he didn't have to carry me, this was going to be a tougher sell. I sagged down the fender.

"Sasha!" He dropped the crutches, my bag slipped, and his hand gripped my upper arm. Leaning awkwardly to keep from dropping the rest, he pressed me against the car and shut the door. I almost felt bad.

But then his fingers brushed the curve of my breast and his breath fanned my face. Butterflies erupted in my stomach and I couldn't believe I'd wasted so much time on a stupid rule. My lids lowered and I looked at him from beneath the fan of my lashes.

He mumbled something incoherent and stuck his other arm through my backpack. Clearly, he wasn't buying it just yet, but I knew I could convince him once we were inside.

The heavy books shifted, tugging him backward. "How much shit do you have in here?"

Readjusting the weight and leaning my crutches against the car, he scooped me up.

I sighed and linked my arms around his neck. He jerked when my nails scratched gently against his skin. I tried not to giggle. This was the first time I'd ever played the flirt to this extreme. Even with the drugs, I was having fun. Before he saw me and thought I was teasing, I tucked my head beneath his chin.

He grunted and shifted me. My fingertips slid higher until his rapid pulse pounded beneath my fingertips. While he might not be saying much, his body was answering. I unclasped my hands and twisted the knob. Carefully, he bent us around the door, easing me into the living room. Leaning one shoulder against the wall, he inched his shoulders out of my backpack and let it slide to the floor.

"You need more books." He shrugged his shoulders and lifted me higher.

He kicked the door shut with his heel and headed toward the couch. I was running out of time. Our last sofa time had gone well enough, but I didn't want those memories messing up tonight. I yawned. "Put me down here and I'll walk to my room."

He tightened his grip. Rolling waves of heat shot up my thighs and I bit my lip. He stared straight ahead, face impassive. If he didn't have a death-grip on my thighs, I'd think I was nothing more than a guitar bag.

"Wait!" I spread my hands along the hallway.

He stopped and looked down. Frustration and anger and lust mingled together on his face. This experiment of mine was either going to go horribly wrong, or horribly right.

"I need my iPod. It's in the side pocket of my backpack."

He craned his neck and glared at the bag. "Are you sure?"

I waited for him to turn back to me. My gaze roamed his face. I'd never noticed his crooked five o'clock shadow. One side curled almost to the edge of his nostril, but the other was low around the corner of his lip. I traced the curve of his lower lip with my eyes, then upward. Most of the anger had burned out, leaving only smoldering lust.

"You could always sing to me."

He blinked and his Adam's apple bobbed in his throat.

Turning slowly, he marched us back to my bag. Then he took a deep breath and squatted, keeping me pressed tightly against his chest.

I fumbled with the bag and pulled my iPod free. "Got it." I tried not to be hurt by his overt rejection. I'd done it to him more than once. Nothing about tonight was going to be easy, and I knew it.

He grunted and stood, rocking up on his tiptoes. I pressed my fingertips into the door to level us out. We retreated back to my room, and he paused on the threshold. My room was pretty subdued compared to the rest of the apartment. Bed, nightstand, single picture of my mom. Survey complete, he stepped inside and stopped.

Afraid he'd bolt once he put me down, I kept my fingers linked around his neck. "Can you set me on the bed. My ankle's really killing me tonight."

"Sure." The strain in his voice was nearly comical. I think if he could've guaranteed a landing, he'd have tossed me from the door. Thankfully, I'd made my bed this morning in some strange karmic preamble, and there weren't any random pairs of panties scattered around the floor like usual.

He lowered me to my handmade quilt and my hips dipped into the over-soft mattress. With one tug, I rolled and pulled him down beside me. He arched his hips and braced his arms like I was in a full-body cast. Luckily, I'd been planning my sneak attack since the door, so my cast was well out of the way of his flailing body parts.

"Sasha, what are you—"

I pressed our bodies together and kissed him again. This time I didn't ease into it. I nipped his lower lip and swiped my tongue across his lips, asking him not nearly as patiently as he'd done.

One hand brushed my cheek and he lowered himself to the mattress. His hands swept into my hair and he cradled my face, tipping me and responding. Our tongues swirled together and he drew mine deep into his mouth. I moaned and he skimmed my neck with his fingers. Mine dipped beneath the hem of his shirt and his abs jumped when I touched them. I wanted to make up for all our lost time.

He kissed my cheeks, and my eyes, nibbled my ear and scored my neck lightly with his teeth. "Sasha," he whispered, tasting my ear.

I moaned and arched against him. His hand found my breast, circling and kneading gently. His head dropped to my cleavage, kissing me through my shirt. I wiggled it upward and in seconds he had us both nearly naked from the waist up. Karma blessed me again with a clean sexy bra instead of my Grannie one that I have to use because I hate laundry. He fingered the blue lace and traced the pink ribbon along the top. "This is nice."

"Mmm." So was the side of his neck. I rubbed my cheek against the stubble and followed with my tongue.

His head dipped low and he took one nipple in his mouth. I grabbed handfuls of his hair. Fingers traced my ribcage and I squirmed. His warm tongue tasted my other nipple and his thumb slipped beneath the lace, rubbing my hard peak.

I rolled closer and brushed the smooth planes of his chest, dipping my finger into the crevice between them and tracing the lines of his abs. He sucked air through his teeth and his mouth froze on my nipple.

"You feel so good," I murmured, letting my hands travel northward again.

He slid a finger beneath my bra strap and tugged it over my shoulder, then unclipped it and tossed it over his head. "Oh Sasha." He cradled both my breasts in his hands and I arched my back. He rolled me onto my back and eased between my thighs. While he caressed and suckled me, I closed my eyes and threaded my fingers through his hair and along his jaw. He hummed that song I could never get out of my head, and the vibrations tickled.

His mouth traveled lower but he never stopped humming. By the time his fingers slipped behind my knees and he situated them over his shoulders, I'd never be able to listen to that song without getting wet.

CHAPTER 9

I made him stop before we had sex, and only because it was four in the morning and my eyes were dropping closed. I didn't want all my hard work dashed when I fell asleep in the middle. A complete gentlemen in bed, like everywhere else, he didn't press me, but cradled me against his chest and pulled the blanket over us.

Then he sang me to sleep. I didn't recognize the song at first, then I realized it was a Journey cover that he'd tweaked. I liked it.

"I think you should sing that at the concert."

"I'd rather sing it to you every night in bed."

I smiled and cuddled closer, sliding my good leg over his thigh. "But it's good."

"And my other stuff?"

I felt him tense beneath my cheek. My answer was important to him. I tried not to think of when I'd been here before. Luckily, this time the answer was easy—and true. "It's good." I tilted my head so he could see my eyes. "I'm serious. You're incredibly talented. And I should know."

He smiled and brushed the hair off my forehead, then kissed the top of my head. "That means a lot."

We cuddled and he stroked my hair. "I should go. Kerri's going to kill me for not bringing her car back."

I reached across him and swiped my phone. Three texts. "Oops." I twisted and snugged my butt into his side and texted her back, then doused the lamp and plugged my phone in. He curled against me and tucked his arm around my waist. My pink cast was a giant lump under the covers, but he gently eased himself around it.

We slept spooned together until my alarm bleeped at six. I nudged him awake with kisses. "Hey."

He nuzzled my neck. "Good morning."

"I have to go to class. Since you have Ker's car, will you drop me?"

"Is she pissed?"

I fumbled for my phone again and checked. "No. But we have to grab her before class."

His hand found my breast and he pulled me tight against him. "Last night was—"

I sighed. "Amazing."

"Please tell me it wasn't a dream. I'm warning you though, I can't go back. Not now."

I rolled over and cupped his face between my hands. "Only forward."

He kissed me slow and deep, stealing the promise from my body. My snooze broke us apart and I grimaced. "I could stay like this all day but we have that lit test."

"And I have a ton of stuff before the concert. What time will I see you?"

"Kerri and I will be there at three."

He kissed me again. "Perfect."

We showered and dressed, then grabbed Kerri. It was the longest day of my entire life. I swear a few times the clock went in reverse.

Kerri met me outside of the English building and I raced across the sidewalk, finally getting the hang of my three-legged hobble. I climbed in and Kerri's grin was infectious.

She grabbed my crutches and angled them into the back seat. "Well?"

I leaned my head back. "Ohmigosh, Ker. You were right." I squeezed her hand. "You're always right. Forgive me?"

She kissed the back of my hand, squealed, and catapulted herself into my seat, squishing me in a giant hug. "I'm so happy for you guys!"

I hugged her back and spit out a mouthful of her hair. "Okay, okay. Let's go so I can see him."

She jerked and popped back into her seat, jamming the car into drive. "Right. I've got stuff with me, so let's go to your place."

I could barely sit still. Kerri did my hair and makeup while I fidgeted with how to make pants work over my cast. I settled on a way-too-short skirt and lace top over a red tank. I had *groupie* written all over me. And I loved it.

We giggled and carried on with ridiculous glee, then sprinted to the arena as fast as I could get there. Jesse met us at Will Call with tickets, backstage passes, and an embarrassingly thorough hey-there kiss. I straightened and fixed my mussed hair. My lips were already swollen from the kiss and I actually blushed. People flowed around us, some of them grumbling, and a few of the girls made heaving sighing noises. Dating a musician had its perks.

"Okay, do you guys want to watch us from backstage, or out front?"

Kerri and I traded glances. She fidgeted and tapped one of my crutches. "These would be badass in a moshpit, but I'm not sure it's the best idea."

I grimaced. She was totally right but I wanted to experience Jesse tonight like I had that first night—bombarded by his lyrics and music. Backstage was for pantiless groupies, and I really wanted to watch him sing.

"You've got seats, so there might be less bumping and ramming. They're not great seats though." His face fell. I think he thought he'd let us down.

I squeezed against him. "It's all good. Is there a spot backstage where I can watch you?"

His face exploded in a huge grin. "Absolutely." He turned me around and slipped a lanyard over my head, then lifted my hair over the string. When his fingers brushed my skin, a streak of heat raced down my spine.

Kerri put hers on and winked at me, then we made our way through the crowd and into the VIP section. Security gave me grief about my crutches, but a supervisor finally let us through. Jesse was stressing about the time.

I tugged him to a stop. "It's going to take me a minute to get through these bodies. Go and we'll be there before your set starts. I promise."

Conflicted emotions warred on his face. I knew his chivalry wouldn't let me battle this alone.

"I have Kerri."

She flared her elbows and set her face in her best bouncer-face. "I got this."

He laughed and hugged us both. "I'm so glad you're here." His hands lingered on my face, then he bolted.

I jerked my chin toward the crowd. "Part the seas."

"Excuse me! Cripple, coming through."

We laughed the entire way. Nothing could ruin tonight for me. Nothing.

It took some finagling and flirting, but we finally made our way past security and to stage left. I waved and Jesse rushed over. "We're almost on." He kissed me.

"Break a leg."

He grinned and yelled at the security guard. "Get her a stool, will ya?"

The guy scowled, then saw my cast.

"She'll let you sign it," Kerri said in her best sing song voice.

His face softened and he disappeared, reappearing in a few seconds with two stools. Kerri and I scooted as close as we could to the stage as the drummer tapped out their intro. My heart swelled as Jesse's syrup-smooth voice wrapped around me. Now that I'd let my past go, I could finally enjoy his music and talent without bias. He'd been good before, but I'd viewed him through tainted lenses. Tonight, nothing stood between my appreciation for pure talent.

Maybe my past wouldn't be such a hindrance. I did have an awful lot of contacts that could help a guy like Jesse. But they still had to get rid of that bass player. My head jerked up when Jesse pointed at me.

"If you guys don't mind, I'd like to bring someone special out for this next number."

"Oh no, he didn't," Kerri whispered.

I think he did. I was still too stunned to speak as he walked across the stage to thunderous applause. I shook my head. "I don't want to go out there," I hissed.

He grinned and took my hand, then scooped me up. "Grab the stool," he shouted over his shoulder to the security guard.

The applause increased and people whistled and I think someone shouted my name. Jesse settled me on the stool and I shot Kerri a pleading look. She held up her hands and shrugged.

"Everybody, this is Sasha."

"Hi Sasha!" The entire arena shouted.

"I wasn't going to sing this next song, but Sasha here convinced me I should." He strummed his guitar. "I hope you guys like it."

He grabbed another stool from in front of the drum set and sat at an angle to me and the crowd.

My eyes teared and I swallowed as he sang the first notes of last night's ballad. Everyone else fell away, and it was the two of us, sitting alone on that stage. Every lyric embedded itself on my heart.

The song ended and he kissed me to another wild round of applause, then took a bow and carried me off the stage.

Kerri stood and applauded the loudest.

We gathered my crutches and moved into the hallway behind the stage filled with bands and bodies. I couldn't stop grinning. Jesse set me down and helped me balance. The crowd grew and swarmed. One of the bigger bands must have been headed our way. If we didn't get out of there quickly, it was going to be tough. I wasn't *that* good on crutches yet.

"I told the guys I'd pack if they tore down, so we could go around to our seats and watch the other bands."

I kissed him. "Tonight was amazing."

"Better than last night?"

"Two hundred percent."

He grinned and spun me around, whispering against my ear. "Wait until I sing the rest of tonight's songs."

I blushed and looked up to navigate my way. The crowd parted for the next band headed onstage.

I doubled over like someone punched me.

Before me stood the only man I'd ever loved. The one who'd crushed my heart and never looked back. The reason I hated musicians for all time.

He grinned and reached for me. "Hey, princess."

"Hi, dad."

About the Author

After earning a master's degree in secondary education from UNC, Elizabeth Nelson worked abroad teaching English, bar-tended at late night clubs in Chicago, and continues various philanthropy projects that focus on empowering women. But her love of writing never changed.

Want to see what happens next with Sasha and Jesse? <u>Backstage Pass: VIP is now available!</u>

Sasha knows what kind of heartbreak can accompany a talented rock star's relationships. But she finds herself falling for one nonetheless—the way he falls in with her rhythm is mesmerizing and addicting. And when a family emergency sends her running home, there's no one she wants by her side but lead singer and new boyfriend Jesse.

When she learns about her parents' relationship—or lack thereof—will this new information quell Sasha's fears or only rekindle old questions that continue to resurface? She knows Jesse isn't her dad, and she's not her mom, but her long held stereotypes of dating rock stars are hard to break.

Jesse does his utmost to prove to Sasha that he's worth fighting for and breaking her own rules for. Will he continue to be a picture of love, loyalty and strength, or will everything Sasha believes come true at the worst possible time?

Other Books by Elizabeth Nelson

Backstage Pass

Backstage Pass: VIP

Backstage Pass: All Access

Backstage Pass: Behind the Music

Backstage Pass: On Tour

Backstage Pass: Last Call

***

You Only Live Once 1

You Only Live Once 2

You Only Live Once 3

You Only Live Once 4

You Only Live Once 5

***

Curiosity Killed the Kat

The Game is On

A Date with the Devil

***

Forbidden Love

Forbidden Desire

Forbidden Decision

***

1st Chance

2nd Chance

3rd Chance

***

Trinity

Desire

Unconditional

***

Cautious

***

Behind Closed Doors – Alaska

Behind Closed Doors – Nashville

Behind Closed Doors – Across State Lines

Made in the USA
San Bernardino, CA
19 March 2016